MIXED COMPANY

Praise for *Mixed Company*

"Jenny Shank's *Mixed Company* is a masterfully-written short story collection full of insight and stunning humor. You will never forget these gritty, real characters: Davonya running for her life, the mother-in-law who lost her legs by throwing herself in front of a train, "La Sexycana," and so many more. In this courageous exploration of place, race, and survival, *Mixed Company* is a book to read and reread in utter delight."

—Erika Krouse, author of *Come Up and See Me Sometime*

Ms. Ardis C. Nelson
PO Box 513
Annandale, MN 55302

Mixed Company

Stories

Jenny Shank

Texas Review Press
Huntsville, Texas

Published by Texas Review Press
Huntsville, TX

Names: Shank, Jenny, 1976- author.
Title: Mixed company : stories / Jenny Shank.
Description: Huntsville : Texas Review Press, [2021] |
"2020 Winner of the George Garrett Fiction Prize."
--ECIP title page verso.
Identifiers: LCCN 2021017016 (print) |
LCCN 2021017017 (ebook) | ISBN
9781680032611 (paperback) | ISBN 9781680032628 (ebook)
Subjects: LCSH: Relationship quality--Colorado--Denver--Fiction. |
Denver (Colo.)--Social life and customs--Fiction. | |
Denver (Colo.)--Fiction. |
LCGFT: Short stories. | Domestic fiction.
Classification: LCC PS3619.H35469 M59 2021 (print) |
LCC PS3619.H35469
(ebook) | DDC 813.008/035878883--dc23
LC record available at https://lccn.loc.gov/2021017016
LC ebook record available at https://lccn.loc.gov/2021017017

Author Photo: Maya Chastang
Cover and Interior Design: Bradley Alan Ivey

Epigraph on page viii © 2021 The Andy Warhol Foundation for
the Visual Arts, Inc. / Licensed by Artists Rights Society (ARS), New
York

2020 Winner of the George Garrett Fiction Prize

For Julien, Maya, and Theo

Ghetto space is wrong for America. It's wrong for people who are the same type to go and live together. There shouldn't be any huddling together in the same groups with the same food. In America it's got to mix 'n' mingle. If I were President, I'd make people mix 'n' mingle more. But the thing is America's a free country and I couldn't make them.

—Andy Warhol, *The Philosophy of Andy Warhol* (1975)

Contents

L'homme de ma vie

On my wedding day, I realized I didn't know my mother-in-law's name. I'd never met her, and Etienne rarely spoke of her. Her name was—is—Véronique. The gap in my husband's family didn't really bother me until we had the kid, a couple of years after we married. When the kid was two, we brought her from Colorado to Paris to meet Etienne's great-aunt Adélaïde, the woman who'd taken care of him as a baby after the first time Véronique tried to kill herself.

The day we arrived in Paris we dragged ourselves around in the wind, trying to stay awake before we visited Tante Adélaïde. Intermittent rain stung our faces. We staggered from our hotel past the Grand Palais over the Pont Alexandre III.

"I wish we could stay with Adélaïde," Etienne said. "That would be simpler."

"She's eighty-five," I said.

"And her apartment is too small," he agreed. When he was single, he'd slept at her place, knees tucked up on a stiff canapé. But there were three of us now.

The poor jet-lagged kid, slouched in her stroller, kept saying, "Little problem. Little problem." She furrowed her brow, not knowing why she felt so funny, wanting us to do something for her. When Etienne checked on her, she switched languages and continued to implore, *Petit problème*. It made me proud and mystified to be raising a French girl in Colorado, and to bring her to Paris and hear her speaking with the same accent as all the other little girls in colorful tights.

"My mom's apartment, on the other hand," Etienne said, "is huge."

I tried to picture it. Would it be filled with prints and sculptures and uncomfortable antique furniture, like Tante Adélaïde's place? Maybe Véronique didn't have seats for guests. With no legs, she wouldn't need them.

"Nicole," Etienne said, looking out over the gray-green expanse of the Seine, "I want both of you to come with me to see my mother."

In the half-dozen times I'd visited Paris with Etienne, he'd never let me meet Véronique. "Sure," I said, "if that's what you want." I was eager to see Véronique at last, but I wondered if the kid was still baby enough not to notice the many things that were wrong with her.

When I was pregnant and too uncomfortable to sleep, in the middle of the night while the baby thrashed inside me, I searched the internet for statistics on schizophrenia. People with no schizophrenic relatives had a one percent chance of developing the disease; people with one schizophrenic grandparent had a five percent chance. That quintupling of the kid's odds scared me. We wouldn't know if she had it until she was twenty-five or thirty, when women typically showed symptoms. But scientists thought the environment triggered whether a susceptible person developed the disease. The old theory that a cold, uncaring "refrigerator mother" caused schizophrenia was discredited, but studies suggested a positive family environment cut the chances. Isolation and abuse increased the chances. So I was knocking myself out trying to give the kid a happy childhood. There would be pony rides. There would be ice cream. Growing up in Colorado provided near-perpetual sunshine and a can-do Western attitude. Exposure to her legless grandmother who thought her dad was still eight years old wasn't part of the plan.

We saw the Eiffel Tower in the distance and the kid pointed and shouted, *"Tour Eiffel!"* Etienne kissed her curly head and said,

"*Bravo!*" He'd filled our house with miniature replicas of the Eiffel Tower. The kid said "*Tour Eiffel!*" whenever she spotted ugly power-line towers back home in Denver, too.

We tucked the kid in for a nap and turned on the TV. TF1 was playing an episode from Kieslowski's *Dekalog*, the one where the young woman finds a letter from her dead mother saying the man who raised her wasn't her father.

"My mom told me that once," Etienne said.

I usually found out about Etienne's mother when we were watching some movie depicting a messed-up family situation. "How old were you?" I asked.

"I must have been about seven. Before the second time she tried to kill herself."

I only asked about Véronique when Etienne brought her up, so now was my chance. "Do you think it's true?"

"My dad denied it. I know it's not true. I look like my dad."

Whenever Etienne mentioned something horrible that was said or done to him as a child, I pictured him as a boy and shuddered. How could any mother could treat her child that way?

When Véronique was pregnant with Etienne, they moved from Paris to New York where his father took a job with IBM. Véronique spoke only French and knew no one. She had her first breakdown after Etienne was born. I wondered if the isolation in New York was the crucial domino that knocked all her bad genes into place. She tried to kill herself for the first time when Etienne was three weeks old, driving her car into a tree and ending up with a broken jaw.

After Véronique's suicide attempt, Tante Adélaïde, Etienne's father's aunt, traveled from France to raise him for the first six months. I knew what that meant—endless giving on no sleep, piles of diapers, vomit in your hair, poop under your fingernails, crying jags, feeding, bouncing, singing, rocking, until the baby finally dropped off, then lying awake to listen to him breathe. Adélaïde had done that for Etienne. We'd named the kid for her: Adèle.

Véronique was stable when Adélaïde left Etienne and returned to Paris. Etienne's dad tried to send him to kindergarten, but Véronique would walk three miles to school, barefoot, and tell the teacher he was sick. He missed so many classes, the teacher put him in special ed and sent him to the nurse for an evaluation every time his mom appeared. Once when Véronique refused to let him leave the house, Etienne's dad hid him in the trunk of the car and drove him to school.

"Was Véronique ever well?" I asked.

"Not since I was born. But there were times when she was steadier and she'd cook for me. I loved her cherry *clafoutis*."

I could almost taste Véronique's buttery, flan-like *clafoutis*. Terrible that this was the one good thing anyone could remember her creating.

"Mostly she'd just stand in the kitchen and chain smoke," Etienne said, "rocking from side to side, muttering. When my dad was at work, I'd hide in my room or outside."

Outside, Etienne roamed nature, teaching himself botanical terms, and now he called out the names of trees and flowers like he was greeting old friends. In Colorado, we hiked for hours, Etienne's mood lightening with every mile on the trails, our daughter strapped to his back in the sunshine.

I wished someone who'd loved Véronique, who'd known her before she'd lost it, could make her real for me. Instead, when I thought of her, a flare of irrational anger for Etienne's neglect would rise. "What was she like before you?" I asked.

Etienne shrugged. "I wasn't there." His eyes went glassy as he lost himself in reliving his miserable childhood, something I could never understand, even though I tried.

I shouldn't have prodded him about Véronique. My own mom was the opposite of mysterious, loving to a fault. She was always saving coupons for me, offering to babysit, taking the midnight shift when the kid was a newborn, sending me home with garden tomatoes and banana bread when I visited, lining up the little journals that printed my stories on a shelf in my old bedroom like a monument to me. "It's because of you," I'd tell her, "that I have nothing to write about." Etienne said he thought about his mother every day, and sometimes I'd try to guess if the horror show was playing in his mind, when a certain abstracted look came over him, or when he took too long to answer a question.

Etienne was eight the second time Véronique tried to kill herself. She was returning from outpatient treatment at a White Plains psychiatric center when she threw herself in front of a Metro North train. Her legs were severed, but she didn't bleed to death because the train cauterized her wounds.

After the kid woke from her nap we walked over to Tante Adélaïde's. We knocked on her door and she flung it open, saying, *"Salut, mes enfants!"* I held up the kid, who buried her face in my neck. She wore a navy sailor dress, and in the Paris humidity her hair curled up like Shirley Temple's. I'd never been so proud of anything as I was of her, and she hadn't even done much yet. Adélaïde kissed my cheeks three times, going from one to the other. I never knew which cheek to start with. *"Comment ça va, Nicole?"* she asked. My name sounded more sophisticated in French. Nee-col.

"*Mais très bien, merci.*" Adélaïde spoke little English, and I'd studied French in the seven years since I met Etienne. We wanted the kid to speak French so that Etienne would have at least one native speaker to talk to when his family was gone. "Teaching her French feels like a matter of life and death for me," he'd told me once. Lately, I'd found that French was a good language to mother in. I told the kid extravagant things, *I adore you, my little cabbage,* that in French did not sound weird, even when I declared this to her as she sat in a grocery cart in the middle of the produce department. I liked French picture books too, depicting bananas speckled with brown spots instead of the unblemished yellow peels of those in American storybooks.

Adélaïde wore her silver hair swept up, a sweater pinned with a cameo brooch, and a long skirt. She was formal, displeased with Parisians pronouncing *oui* as *way* instead of *wee*. She'd worked at the Bibliothèque Nationale for forty years as a librarian specializing in Voltaire. She'd written many papers, including one she'd published only a few years earlier about the illustrated versions of *Candide*. She led us past the bust of Voltaire—*l'homme de ma vie*, she called him. The man of my life.

Adélaïde had lived in the same apartment for fifty years, moving there with her divorced mother just after World War II, and taking care of her until she died. She never married. Etienne said she'd had a suitor once, but her mother scared him off.

Tante Adélaïde's sitting room was stuffed with artifacts from her years as a librarian—rare books and Voltaire journals—as well as decorative medals, figurines, and porcelain replicas of eighteenth-century plates. Unchecked, the kid would reduce it to shambles in five minutes. Adélaïde wanted Adèle to sit on a chair with a stiff back and carved wooden legs, which she did for about two seconds before she wriggled down.

"*J'ai rêvé d'elle assise sur mes genoux*," Adélaïde said. She'd dreamed of Adèle sitting on her knees. For some reason, the term "lap" didn't exist in the French language. When I thought about it, a lap was an imaginary thing. Which countries had laps and which didn't?

Adélaïde dabbed at her eyes with a lace handkerchief. "It's very moving for your old Adélaïde to meet *la petite* Adèle." The kid sat in her great-great aunt's lap and Adélaïde shook her head gently, stroking Adèle's curls with a thick-knuckled hand. "She has your *retroussé* nose," she told Etienne. She kissed Adèle on the turned-up nose that matched Etienne's, which he told me was a copy of Véronique's. Three generations, at least, in one nose. I often wondered if any of Véronique's other features had filtered down to the kid. But Etienne didn't have or want any photographs of his mother.

Tante Adélaïde gave the kid a little red wooden horse from Sweden. She took the horse and flitted in and out among the gauzy curtains by the window. Etienne coaxed Adèle into displaying her French, holding up pictures and figurines around the room for her to name. *Cheval. Vache. Tortue. Papillon.* For a Colorado kid, she had a good French accent, putting some native throat gargle into her r's.

"She speaks French perfectly!" Adélaïde exclaimed, clapping her hands together. "She'll be reading Voltaire soon."

"She's already finished *Candide*," I said.

Adélaïde laughed. "How are your literary endeavors progressing?"

I shrugged and made this little insouciant noise with a pursed mouth that in French meant: *who knows?* I tried to write, and Adélaïde took it seriously, the way a mother would. A writer struggling over his work without succeeding in publishing a book was considered a sort of romantic hero in France, whereas in the U.S., such a person was seen as a type of bum.

"I wouldn't call what I do literature," I said.

"But you are published!" Adélaïde cried.

But I am published! I wanted to have this printed on a T-shirt. At Adélaïde's insistence, I'd sent her a copy of a journal with one of my stories, a tale about Bigfoot, set in the Wind River Range of Wyoming. Adélaïde had sat down with her friend Hugette, who taught English to *lycéens,* and translated the story, then wrote me a fervid letter of praise, noting my rugged images of nature. The French were big on the romance of the American West. Etienne's family got a kick out of it when I wore my cowboy hat.

"*Avez-vous faim, mes enfants?*" she asked.

"*Faim!*" the kid said, *hungry!*

Adélaïde's mother had done the cooking so she didn't have to try until she was past fifty. I dreaded trying to choke down her weird stewed meats. I was a picky eater, but I was raising the kid to be better than me: she'd been eating fish since she could chew, and whenever Etienne brought home something pungent and French—a moldy cheese or a paté—I had Adèle try it.

I was relieved when Adélaïde set out a brioche for the kid and patisseries for us, wrapped in pretty triangles of paper, *babas au rhum, religieuses, millefeuilles, tartes, éclairs au café.* Only in Paris did I eat two cakes in place of dinner. I took one bite of something marvelous, filled with cloud-light cream, before I had to chase the kid into the other room. I brought her back, wriggling. It made me sad she was so young and Adélaïde was so old; this was the closest she'd ever come to having a paternal grandmother and she probably wouldn't even remember. If Adèle did retain a memory from this trip, I hoped it would be of this—sweets for dinner in Tante Adélaïde's kitchen—and not of whatever she saw at Véronique's apartment. Maybe the trick to achieving a happy childhood was providing the right ratio—say, ten good experiences for every one bad?

I scraped the cream from Adèle's cheek into her mouth with a spoon. She took the spoon from me and dug into the éclair on my plate, handing me her slobbery brioche. "Who fed you when you were a boy?" I asked Etienne.

"My mom did, when she wasn't in the hospital."

"What did you usually eat for dinner?"

"I remember her making rice."

"Plain rice? That's it?"

"And peeled grapes. She would peel every grape."

Adélaïde shook her head. "That's no way to feed a child. You're not going to see her, are you?"

"Maybe tomorrow," Etienne said.

"*Merde!*" Adélaïde yelled, bringing her fist down on the table, causing some of her porcelains to jump next to the magnifying glass that she used for reading. "What's the point of seeing her?" Adélaïde, like everyone in his father's family, didn't understand why he tried to maintain contact with his mother. No one in his mother's family—who were bitter at Etienne's father over the divorce—had ever tried to become involved in his life.

"You're probably right," Etienne said.

"Here's something for *la petite*," she said, handing me an envelope. "Some old family photos Adèle might want," she explained. She gave Etienne a black jewelry box.

Etienne opened it to find a small medal attached by a silver laurel wreath to a blue ribbon. Blue and silver points emanated from the center, which bore the profile of Marianne, the female symbol of France, and the words *Republique Française*. Adélaïde explained it was a miniature version of a medal the government awarded her for working at the Bibliothèque Nationale for forty years, and she produced the larger one to show us.

"But it's for Adèle?" Etienne asked.

"*Mais oui!*"

I was intrigued that Adélaïde had a main medal plus a mini backup one. I asked Adélaïde if she wore her medal, and she laughed. But I was serious. I liked to think that if I'd been born French, I'd have won a medal for something. God knows what. But if I had, I'd wear it. Every day.

"*C'est un geste très affectueux*," Etienne said, "but we can't accept it."

"*Mais oui oui oui oui oui*," she insisted.

I put my hand on his arm to stop him from handing the box back. Adèle would never receive a present from her own grandmother. This would be something to keep for when she was older, after Adélaïde was gone, to show that she'd been loved. Besides, I liked to think of our daughter back in Colorado, running on the playground and wearing her little blue medal for forty years of service as a French librarian.

"It's Adèle's first trip to Paris!" Adélaïde said. "Skip visiting Véronique and go somewhere joyful tomorrow—the Jardin du Luxembourg."

Etienne looked up at her, the closest figure to a mother he'd ever had, and nodded. "*Bonne idée*," he agreed, while I sank back in my chair, relieved for Adèle, but wondering if I'd ever meet his mother.

That night TF1 was showing the 1948 version of *Anna Karenina*, starring Vivien Leigh, dubbed into French. I first read the Tolstoy book when Etienne and I had been dating for about a year, and he touched the cover and said, "So, you're reading *that*." He'd never read it but knew what happened to Anna at the end.

Vivien Leigh's French voice was too deep. We kept the volume low so we wouldn't wake the kid and talked over the black and white images flickering in the dark room.

"When you see a person with a missing arm or leg, what do you feel?" Etienne asked.

"Compassion," I said. "I say a prayer for the person inside my head."

"I feel terrorized."

I had seen him inch away from people in wheelchairs, or simply turn his back.

"Bellevue was horrifying," Etienne continued, his face glowing in the television's light. "There were people who'd been in the worst accidents imaginable, patients in traction, four to a room. She went crazier after the second time she tried to kill herself, and she knew the stumps of her legs frightened me, so she'd purposely try to scare me, grabbing me by the shoulder and waving the stumps at me until I screamed and ran away."

In childbirth preparation class, the nurses showed us the room that would be used for a cesarean. Unlike the deluxe hotel accommodations of the recovery rooms, it had medical machines and instruments everywhere, and Etienne could barely enter it before he ducked back into the hall. He'd spent too much of his childhood sitting in such a room in Bellevue, forced to visit someone who didn't even live in this world. "If I need a C-section," I'd told him, "you don't have to watch."

Etienne fell asleep before I was tired, so I took out the photos from Adélaïde. I had no idea who the people in the early black-and-white photos were: a dapper man in a military uniform with a curled black moustache, a boy dressed like Little Lord Fauntleroy perched on his knee, a nanny in a starched black dress and white cap holding a baby dressed in puffy layers of pale lace, the streets of Paris in 1910, flooded to the height of the bridges. There were a few more recent pictures from the '60s, including one of Etienne's dad when he was in his twenties, slimmer, with thicker hair, his arm around a beautiful woman who must have been Véronique.

I sat up in bed and turned on another light to see better. She was tall and slender like Etienne, with auburn hair, the color nothing like the kid's ash blonde curls. But she had their turned-up nose, a smattering of freckles across the bridge. How could you not love someone with that nose? I stared at the photo. She seemed healthy, vibrant. I tucked this photo into the novel I was reading so Etienne couldn't destroy it. I would keep it for Adèle in case she ever wanted to see her grandmother's face.

The next day at the Jardin du Luxembourg, the magnolia trees were in bloom and we lifted the kid into the blossoms. The sun came out and people basked in the park, sitting on green metal chairs around fountains, propping their legs. Parisians took off their coats and opened the tops of their shirts and leaned back their heads and relaxed. I imagined Véronique, locked in her apartment in the middle of this beautiful city, never enjoying Paris.

In the Grand Bassin, ducks and fish swam among little wooden sailboats. Etienne said if a boat ever got stuck in the middle of the pond, someone would take two chairs and construct a moving bridge to fetch it. We considered renting a boat for Adèle, but she didn't have the patience yet.

"Rent one," I told Etienne. His love for Paris was a perpetual ache in his heart. His only happy childhood times had been here, when he came to spend the summers with Adélaïde and his grandparents, far away from his mother in New York. I wanted him to do all the things he missed. "I can chase her."

"And play with the boat all by myself?" he asked. "I've done that enough."

A little boy took a stick and poked at an orange fish at the bottom of the basin, its belly to the sun, motionless except for tiny revolutions of one fin. "*Il est mort*," the boy said.

"It's *almost* dead," his dad corrected.

"*Il est presque mort*," the boy repeated gravely.

Adèle walked closer for a look, frowning and furrowing her brow, and I clutched her hand so she wouldn't tumble in. With all the hazards kids are drawn to, I wondered how Etienne survived being watched by Véronique. I'd read mothers with schizophrenia responded to their children inappropriatley, rarely doing what the child needed, smothering the kid with attention when he wanted to be free, shirking him when he wanted comfort. It was the opposite of what most mothers did, mirroring the kid's expressions, echoing her babble, reflecting the baby's emotions so she could learn what it was to feel.

"I once had a pet goldfish named Maxwell," Etienne said, taking Adèle's other hand. "One summer I left for France, and instead of finding someone to take care of it, my mom dumped it in the lake."

"That's terrible," I said. "I wish one of your childhood stories would end with pony rides and ice cream." I considered the kid's happy-day-to-sad-day ratio, calculating how many rides on the carousel I'd have to buy her to make up for the almost-dead fish.

More people gathered near the almost-dead fish and speculated on its health as it swam in a circle on its side with the aid of pathetic little movements of its fins. "*C'est quoi mort?*" Adèle asked her papa as she studied the fish, what is dead?

"*C'est de rêver pour toujours*," he said, lifting her in his arms. It's to dream forever.

That wasn't quite right, but I didn't know what to tell a two-year-old. Dreaming forever was kind of like what Véronique did.

I'd once read that the closest you could come to feeling what it's like to be schizophrenic was in the confused moment between sleeping and waking, when dreams haven't slipped away and you don't know for certain what's real.

We met Tante Adélaïde at Chez Nini, a restaurant where she invited us to eat every time we visited. It was elaborately decorated for a couscous place: white tablecloths, chandeliers, walls with the sinuous curves of Islamic buildings and murals of Bedouins, curio cabinets stuffed with camels, vases of fresh flowers on the tables. Nini, the proprietor, was a stout French woman with short brown hair, ruddy cheeks, and shiny eyes. While she took orders, her Algerian husband did the cooking.

Adélaïde admired the kid's pink western shirt with pearl snap buttons. "*Une petite* cowgirl!" Adélaïde said.

She started us off with sangria, then ordered white wine. "*Nous allons faire la fête*," she declared, "We're going to live it up." She lived on a small pension, but always bought us meals and pressed envelopes of Euros into our hands when we visited.

"I have a present for *la petite*," Adélaïde announced, handing Etienne a cloth-wrapped packet.

"Another one?" Etienne said. "You shouldn't have."

He opened the cloth to find some old silver, including a spoon engraved with the initials Adélaïde and Adèle shared. When Etienne passed it to me, I was surprised by its weight. It was dull and old, like something you'd see in a museum of how people used to live. There were half a dozen spoons and a couple of forks with serrated sides, and Adélaïde explained a superstition that if you ever gave a gift of something that cut, the recipient had to pay for it with money, or it would cut the friendship.

I reached into my pocket and fished out ten Euro cents, or whatever you called them, and passed it to her. I wondered how Europeans tolerated it, having to give up not only their currencies but also their pet names for those currencies, replacing it with these bills and coins that were decorated with fake monuments meant to look only vaguely like real ones. Maybe Europeans had so much history they were bored of it.

In my half-baked French I tried to explain to Adélaïde about how, in the U.S., people got all excited waiting for their state's quarter to appear. "They couldn't do that with the Euro," I speculated, "because the French would resent the quarter with the German beergarten on it." I was going for a joke, but nobody laughed. The look was on Etienne's face again as his tagine arrived, steam rising when he lifted the ceramic dome.

"Why don't you visit your mom tomorrow," I suggested, "to get it over with?"

"Why see her at all?" Adélaïde asked. "She already has your grandmother's apartment. We've all suffered enough because of her."

I kept quiet. I credited Adélaïde's love for how Etienne had become a good man, but I didn't always think she knew what was best for him. He seemed better able to enjoy the rest of the trip after he saw Véronique, as though he'd fulfilled his duty to her, and was freed of the dread of encountering his mother for another two years.

"I know hardly anyone in Paris anymore," Etienne said. He knew all the streets, recited facts about every monument, and could guide us efficiently through all the bus routes and Metro lines, but when Tante Adélaïde was gone there would be no one to visit.

My own family was burgeoning, dozens of aunts, uncles, and cousins spread across the U.S., babies dropping every year so that when we gathered at the old family ranch in Colorado we herded the children into a fenced yard with toys and they formed a sort of pack and played until they passed out. I didn't know what it was like for Etienne or Adélaïde, who had so few people to cling to.

As we ate, Etienne asked Adélaïde about his family members who'd died, trying to store up the stories for Adèle. This was how Etienne's family came to diminish until its last survivor would be our kid: his great-grandfather was called to serve in World War I even though he was forty and the sole breadwinner for his children—maybe he was the moustache guy with the Fauntleroy? He died at Verdun. Without his income, the family lost its chateau in the country and its art-framing business that served the royal family of Monaco, but held on to their apartment in Paris, where Etienne's mother now lived. Adélaïde never married, and her older brother, Etienne's grandfather, had two children. But he was a doctor in the army, and when he was serving in Madagascar during World War II, the war at sea kept supplies from crossing the ocean, leaving them with nothing but mangos and papayas to eat. The baby died of malnutrition. Etienne's father, who was knock-kneed and spindly in pictures from those years, survived to marry a schizophrenic, and the only kid they had was Etienne.

"It's sad, the history of our family," Adélaïde said, signaling an end to the subject. "Have you visited *La Maison de Victor Hugo*?" she asked.

We were drinking a lot of wine. It made me not care about how the kid fidgeted and how often I had to chase her around the restaurant. I let Etienne stay to spend time with Adélaïde. The other patrons were kind, admiring the kid as she ran by, *Quelle jolie cow-girl!* We lingered at the restaurant, sharing *pâte d'amande* and mint tea, Adélaïde full of questions about our plans and lives, offering suggestions for exhibitions to see. Adèle began to fuss—she needed her *sieste* before Etienne was ready to leave. We had to work on the kid's lingering skills if she was going to be properly French.

While Adèle took her nap, Etienne and I lay on our bed and talked.

"How did Véronique end up in her mother-in-law's apartment?" I asked, a little drunk, violating my own policy.

"The three of us moved to Paris when I started high school because medical care was cheaper here. But then my dad figured out we could never live as a family again—she was too unstable. He and I returned to New York, where he started the divorce proceedings. My father's mother let my mom stay in the apartment, out of pity. Plus, my grandma received subsidies from the French government for letting a disabled person live there. My grandma is dead, but Véronique is still in her apartment." He laughed sadly. "The whole thing is fucked up."

"Who takes care of your mother?"

"They've hired a service to deliver meals," he said. "My mother has a trust, money that she got from my dad in the divorce."

"Is there a lot left?"

"Maybe enough for ten more years."

"Then what?"

"Then the state will take the apartment because she won it in the divorce, and they'll use the money to care for her." He looked at the map of Paris that was the only decoration on the wall. It matched the one he'd framed and hung in Colorado. "My family has lived in that apartment for more than a hundred years."

"But if she dies before the trust runs out?" I asked.

"Then I'll inherit the apartment. In France, it's illegal to disinherit your children. Not like in the U.S."

"But they're big on disowning here." I didn't understand why Véronique's entire family acted as though Etienne didn't exist—even his grandparents. Did one of them abuse Véronique as a child? Was that what activated the schizophrenia genes? No one was disowned in my own large family, not even the drunks. They'd come around and you'd hand them a plate of barbecue.

Véronique was sixty years old, missing both legs and her mind. We lived in a cramped condo, and I thought about how much it would be worth to us if she would die soon. My thoughts felt wrong. I'd never wished anyone dead before. But her life seemed no good to her, and a total heartbreak to those around her, with so many resources poured into her endless well of need. Did she even know that *she* existed, let alone her son? When I met her, maybe I'd be better able to understand. The Christmas after Adèle was born, Etienne sent Véronique a photo of the three of us, grinning, to let her know she had a granddaughter. But sending her a letter was like putting a message in a bottle and chucking it into the sea. You did it just to hear the splash.

That evening it rained and we stayed inside, still sluggish from the heavy lunch. *Quai des Orfèvres*, one of the classic '40s French gangster flicks that I loved, was playing on TF1. It was about a determined police detective investigating the murder of a showgirl's lover.

"The day my mom threw herself in front of the train," Etienne said, "I was playing at a friend's house, and a cop drove up. My dad got out of the cruiser and told me, *Ta mère a eu un accident très grave.* I said, 'Did she break both her legs?' He said, 'No.' I said, 'Did she break her arms and legs?' He said, 'No.' And that's all I remember. Later, the cops brought us a paper bag with her clothes. The bloody pants they'd cut off her."

"Next time a cop tries to hand you a paper bag," I said, "run." I looked at my husband—this good man, who went to work every day for us and came home every night and read the kid stories, did the dishes, and rubbed my feet while we watched movies. How did he manage to be sane? I could see why Etienne had run away for college, all the way from Paris, all the way from New York, and didn't stop running until he hit the Rocky Mountains.

The next morning Etienne announced we were going to visit his mother.

"All of us?" I asked.

"I'd like you there."

"We could leave Adèle with Adélaïde."

"Can you imagine how many knicknacks she'd break? I just want to show my mother that I have a family. I want her to meet her granddaughter one time."

He'd always said he didn't want me to have to see Véronique. But he was a papa now, eager to show off the kid, maybe hoping her face—that third-generation nose—would spark something in Véronique, pull her out of a four-decade funk. I dolled up Adèle in a flowered dress with lavender tights, like all the little Parisian girls wore, with red cowboy boots for luck.

Etienne led us to the Metro station. His shoulders stooped and he frowned, a gloomy expression I knew he wasn't even aware he was making. We waited near the tracks as the train arrived, and he held us so tight I could feel his claws through my coat. On the train, the kid sat on my lap and I held Etienne's hand, which was as cold as Adèle's was warm. I pictured Véronique's apartment, the blinds drawn, the air chain-smoked into a haze. For years she'd kept her clothes in open suitcases, as though she'd be leaving soon. She would be raving, legless, a poor soul cursed with an unkillable body. I thought of the beautiful woman in the photo and tried to subtract to conjure up what Véronique looked like today, but it was math I couldn't do. I hoped Adèle wouldn't be frightened. As much as I wanted to finally see Véronique, how was I ever going to balance out the happy-childhood ratio of this day? The sight of *Grand-mère* would be harder to equalize than the almost-dead fish.

The apartment was across the street from the Nation Metro stop. "It's on Avenue du Trône, the only street in Paris that's wider than it is long," Etienne said as he led us up the stairs. He was full of Paris trivia. "They guillotined thousands of people here during the French Revolution."

Pony rides, I thought, *ice cream*. I wanted to delay. Could I really bring Adèle to see Véronique? A good wife would go with her husband. But what would a good mother do? Etienne had said last time he visited Véronique's apartment, she didn't speak to him directly—instead she held a vulgar conversation with an invisible person about her son, whom she still believed was eight years old. "Why did you tell Etienne that I'm a whore?" Veronique had demanded, over and over. Adèle wouldn't understand her grandmother's favorite words—*pute, putain, salope*—different terms for prostitute, whore, or slut. But did that make it okay for her to hear them?

I followed Etienne to the door, gripping the kid's moist little hand in mine as the mini cars and stunted vans and Mobylettes zipped by on the busy street. At the bottom of the building was a lively café. The waitstaff bustled around, the patrons chatted, ate and drank, unaware of the tormented woman who lived upstairs, not thinking about the blood that ran through the streets here two hundred years earlier. I considered ducking in and drinking a carafe of red wine. If Adèle showed any signs of distress, if she cried or hid from Véronique, or if her grandma started shouting about whores and brandishing her stumps, I'd bring the kid here and order profiteroles, stuffed with ice cream.

Etienne pressed the button on the call box outside the apartment building. *"Maman,"* he said, *"C'est ton fils, Etienne."*

I was surprised that he called her *maman*, like a child. But then I'd never heard a French man of any age calling his mother *mère*.

A garbled, husky voice answered back, then faded away. I couldn't make out a word.

"I'm here with my wife and daughter," he said, "your granddaughter. Will you let us in?"

"J'ouvre," she said, "I'll open," and then fell silent. Pigeons cooed and traffic passed. *"Non, je n'ouvre pas,"* she slurred, "Etienne doesn't have a child. You can't trick me!"

"Don't you want to meet them?" he pleaded. I held Adèle behind him and she reached out to touch her papa's hair. He stood there for three minutes and pressed the button again, but Véronique didn't answer.

We retreated and sat on a metal bench. Etienne hugged himself like he was cold. "It's hard to understand her," he said, "because she doesn't have any teeth."

That I didn't know. Every time I learned something new about Etienne's mother, she lost another body part.

"I'm going to try one more time," he said. "We came all this way. You wait here." He stood and glanced back at us. His eyes reminded me of Adèle's when she was frightened. I wanted to tell him to stop torturing himself and forget he ever had a mother, because he had us now. But I was beginning to understand that all of us had a built-in mother homing instinct, whether the woman on the other end of it warranted it or not. This instinct was so strong that almost nothing could kill it, not insanity or separation or death. And so Etienne walked away from us, a *garçon* trying to persuade his *maman* to meet his family.

A well-dressed woman of about Véronique's age stopped to admire Adèle. The woman wore her ash blonde hair in a chignon and a ruby scarf around her throat. She was perfect, except for the faint lines radiating around her mouth that older French women get either from smoking or because the language makes them purse their lips so often. *"Elle est ravissante,"* she declared, she is ravishing.

The mother pride light inside me beamed. *"Merci."*

For a moment I imagined this lovely *dame* as my mother-in-law, the woman who'd given me my family, who lived just inches away, but who I'd never be able to know, never be able to thank for Etienne's existence. What if schizophrenia had never gripped Véronique? Maybe she would have exacting preferences and we wouldn't get along. She would disapprove of my clothes, take offense when I didn't like something she cooked, say I was too *américaine*. But she would dote on Adèle and invite her to visit in the summertime, as Etienne did his grandmother. She would sing Adèle all the little songs that Etienne didn't know because he didn't have a mother, songs he was teaching her from YouTube: *"Dans la forêt lointaine," "Gentil coquelicot," "Savez-vous planter les choux?"* Because of this French grandmother, Adèle would eat the plain yogurt towers called *Petit Suisses*, pouring a mound of sugar on top, and call hopscotch *"escargot."* Instead of the story of the little gingerbread man, she'd read *"Roule Galette,"* about a mouthy, rolling pastry chased by a fox. She would feel she had a complete family and a culture that went centuries farther back than what we knew about my family.

I sat Adèle on my knee and held her hand in mine. She pointed out an *avion* in the sky. Then she hopped down and broke from me before I could grab her. I rose, desperate to catch her before she darted in front of a moped, but she ran straight for her papa, who reached her before I could. He picked her up and buried his nose in her curls. Adèle wanted to press the buttons on the apartment call box, and Etienne guided her chubby finger to the correct ones.

"*Putain!*" called the garbled voice the kid summoned, "Whore! I said to go away!"

I reached for Adèle, but Etienne clung to her.

"*C'est ta mamie,*" it's your grandma, he said as he kissed Adèle's forehead.

"*Mamie?*" Adèle asked the intercom. And then she began to perform, as she did for all grandparents, singing a sweet song Etienne had taught her from the animated film *Le Roi et l'oiseau.* She belted the high notes as she muddled the words and Etienne joined with her, singing, life is a cherry, death is a cherry pit, love is a cherry tree.

"Etienne!" Véronique hissed. "Go to school. Your slut teachers want you."

Etienne released the intercom button suddenly, as though it was hot, silencing his mother's voice. "She thinks I'm the child singing. She won't open the door." He shook his head. "Last time she at least let me in."

"It's okay," I said, knowing it wasn't. I could continue to picture Véronique as she was in that photo, standing straight, almost smiling, an intact person who had given my husband his life. I knew from my late-night research that Adèle carried a nearly exact replica of Véronique's X chromosome, and so she was closer, genetically, to Véronique than to my mother. They were linked, through time and blood, forever. Behind this door that wouldn't open was Adèle's grandmother, a permanently distressed human, as frightened of us as we were of her.

We sank down on the bench. "At least I know she's still alive." He had no idea if anyone would notify him if she died.

I kissed him hard. No one looked, because we were in Paris. Adèle climbed into his lap.

"*Écoute-moi, ma petite,*" he said to her. "Don't forget this city belongs to you as much as it does to any of these people." He nodded toward a group of young women approaching, high-heeled boots clicking against the pavement, vivid scarves blowing back as they strolled. "Your family has lived here for hundreds of years, and even if there's nobody to visit, Paris is still yours."

"*C'est à moi,*" she said. Mine.

"It's the most beautiful city in the world, and it's yours." Etienne took her face in his hands and kissed her on both cheeks.

Adèle's hair was the color of the winter wheat field we'd passed on our way to the Denver airport, and her eyes were the gray of the Paris sky.

We watched the people pass on the street for a while, and then returned to the Metro. Most of the Metro was underground, but at the end of Line 6 it rose above the earth, and Etienne held Adèle up to the window and said, "*Regarde.*" He wanted her to take in all the buildings, the narrow streets, the funny little cars, the advertisements for weight reduction creams and dairy products, the women in heels who walked with their shoulders back, the men smoking in groups on the corner, the old-timers dressed neatly in vests, coats, and caps. As Adèle and Etienne looked out on Paris, I saw that their profiles matched, as did their accents as they murmured to each other. He pressed his hand on hers against the glass. "*Souviens,*" he told her, remember.

Every mother had a mantra to ward off lurking calamity. This was mine: she would not lose her mind. I wouldn't let her. I would save Etienne and Adèle both. I already had the cowboy hat. Adèle would grow, learn, love, venture, and thrive. She was born in Colorado, but she would belong everywhere.

Lightest Lights Against Darkest Darks

When I opened my locker the first day of junior high, I found a bra hanging from the coat hook, its assertive cups the grayish drab of whites washed with darks. I shut the door before anyone saw. Most of the white families left the district when busing began, but my parents stayed, so I came in with the busload of southeast Denver kids that were shipped a half-hour north to Cole Middle School to mix things up every day. The locker partner assignments were meant to encourage cross-town friendships, but that was hard with kids who wouldn't see each other after the bell rang. According to the slip of paper my homeroom teacher had given me, my locker partner was named Arika, and as I studied the combination, trying to memorize it, she brushed past me, flanked by two chattering friends. She opened the locker, snatched the bra out and stuffed it in her backpack like she didn't care who saw.

"Hi," I said, too quiet for her to hear. That morning I'd worn a red bandana through the belt loops of my jeans, a fashion statement I'd read about in *Seventeen*. An eighth grader who caught the bus at the same stop convinced me to take it off. To make me feel better, the eighth grader said that another kid had worn British Knights sneakers to the bus stop and ended up going home when she told him that those were Crip shoes, BK for Blood Killer. As I thought of the bandana, balled in the bottom of my backpack, I hesitated, and Arika walked off without acknowledging me. I placed a few books on the locker's lower shelf, hoping she wouldn't mind if I claimed that as my own.

A guy wearing sagging jeans and a pick in his hair did a slow, stylized walk down the hall, taking wide steps with a hitch in them, shaking his right hand like he was shooting dice. Across the hall, a ghetto blaster wedged in a locker blared "Bring the Noise," filling the corridor with Chuck D's booming baritone. A teacher lingered in a doorway nearby, and I waited for her to put a stop to it, but she just stood there with her arms crossed over her chest like she was guarding the classroom.

By the end of the day I felt exhausted and lonely, and headed into my final class, art, with relief. The classroom was in the farthest corner of the top floor, at such a remove from the rest of the building that it felt like an artist's garret, with huge frosted-glass windows lining one side. Arika sat at a table in the back, but instead of joining her I walked to the front and sat at an empty table. I pictured all my sixth grade friends, scattered across the city, probably enjoying their first days of school. Busing worked like this: from first to third grade I rode the bus to west Denver, where I went to school mostly with Mexican-American kids. From fourth to sixth grade, the same kids were bused to my neighborhood. I'd probably never see most of them again, and only a handful of the kids from my neighborhood showed up on the bus to head north for middle school, probably because over the summer the gang violence in the area had picked up.

The art teacher, Ms. Omber, looked white but acted like she didn't want to be. Petite, with long caramel curls coaxed into semi-dreads, she wore faded jeans so tight they revealed the definition of her crotch. Her leathery skin was permanently tanned, or maybe that was its natural color—it was impossible to say. I, for one, thought she was just white like me but wore it a whole lot easier than I did. She spoke more like the Black people from that part of town, not with a fake accent but an easy, mellow cadence, dropping in a "baby" here and there when she was talking to a student.

Ms. Omber handed out art pencils and blank sheets of newsprint. "You can get any shade you need out of this one Ebony pencil," she said, holding it up. She made us scribble value scales, challenging us to produce one more degree of light or dark when we brought our papers up to her, saying we were finished.

Darnell, a loudmouth who sat in the back, crept up front when Ms. Omber was checking on people's value scales, and began to open the door to the supply room.

"Hey!" Ms. Omber barked, breaking the contemplative silence of the room. "Did I invite you in there?"

Darnell stopped short. "Just need a new piece of paper, Miss." He held up his sheet, which he'd stabbed through the center with a pencil.

"Then you raise your hand to ask," she snapped. "Listen up everybody," she said, turning to look at all of us, "nobody goes into that supply room but me. The district doesn't give me many supplies and I've got to make them last." She walked up to her desk, took a notepad out of the drawer, and held it out to Darnell.

"What's this?"

"Sign your name," she ordered. "It's the mess up sheet. You get one extra piece of paper a semester and that's it."

Darnell had a knack for turning classes into circuses. Spanish earlier that day had ended with the petite Bolivian teacher shouting, "Stop! Back away from my domain!" as Darnell and his friends beat-boxed and danced around her desk, Darnell supplying the bass tones for their rhythm by blowing raspberries into his cupped palm. When Darnell didn't take the pad, Ms. Omber set it down on the desk and pushed it toward him. She closed her hand around pair of metal scissors. A playful look crossed Darnell's face, like he was about to make a crack, but Ms. Omber stared straight in his eyes and plunged the scissors down into the top of the graffiti-scarred wooden desk. I flinched. She left the scissors standing, imbedded. The smirk fell off Darnell's face. He signed his name to the pad.

I sat at the first table, next to Ms. Omber's desk, beside the forbidden supply room door. Some of the guys whispered to me that I should crane my neck when she went inside and see what was back there, but I kept my eyes on my drawing. The only other kid who sat at that table was Reggie, who also drew in his free time, alternating between accurate renditions of glinting convertibles with glittering rims and the latest Air Jordans, precise down to every lace and swoosh. Reggie hadn't had a growth spurt yet, and he looked like the sort of beatific, fiercely groomed Black child featured in sitcoms. He caught hell because of it, so he drew pictures for people out of self-defense.

When I got home that day, I tried to call some of my old friends. I left messages with three different moms but didn't hear back from anybody. I didn't have any homework so until dinner I went up to my room and drew in my sketchbook, working from pictures that I'd ripped out of magazines.

The second day of school I decided to speak to Arika at our locker during a passing period. She already looked like a high schooler, wearing white K-SWISS sneakers and tight acid-washed jeans that showed off her high butt. Her hair was slicked back, and there were two little curls plastered to the side of her face with a product I learned was called Ultra Sheen Hair Dressing when I saw a jar of it left out in the locker room after gym class, open and glistening next to a rat tail comb.

"So," I said to Arika, shifting in my Keds, "You've got art eighth period with Ms. Omber, right?" I figured this was a safe topic.

"Obviously," she said. "Your name's Emily?"

"Yeah." I nodded, eager to make a friend.

She crossed her arms over her chest and stared at me until I dropped my eyes. "Is your mom Black?" she asked.

"No," I said.

"Is your dad Black?" she persisted.

"No."

She gave me a good long look. "You've got the biggest lips for a white person I've ever seen." Then she shut the locker and walked off.

There were so few white kids that light-skinned people were assumed a mix of something unless proven otherwise. I ducked into the bathroom to study my lips before the bell rang. There is no ugly like middle school ugly. My features looked like they were fighting for control of my face, each of them trying to spread out and amass greater territory. My hair was kinked out and my lips were naturally full, but when you added braces and trumpet lessons that left the insides of them cut and swollen, that was a recipe for freak.

Going to that school made me feel like a parody of a white person that a comedian would perform on BET. He'd hitch up his pants a little too high, stiffen his spine, say something clueless and there I'd be, pegged as bait for laughter. This was 1990, and the kids at school were wearing tri-color leather Africa medallions and T-shirts that said, "It's A Black Thang," and I knew I really didn't understand.

The second day of art class, we moved on to drawing lines, trying to change the shade and thickness by increasing or reducing pressure, without raising our pencils.

"Man, who wants to draw lines?" Arika grumbled.

Ms. Omber walked around, complimenting scrawls that we couldn't see the merit of, telling us, "Now that's a line quality line." She turned on the paint-splattered ghetto blaster that sat on her desk and played old R&B while we drew, now and then telling us who we were listening to: Curtis Mayfield with the Impressions, Ruth Brown, and one song in which a sad man with a trembling voice advised people to take love while they could find it. Ms.

Omber hummed as she worked, stapling white butcher paper to a large bulletin board at the back of the room.

"What are you going to put up there?" Darnell asked.

"Masterpieces," she said.

The music calmed even the rowdiest among us. The last half of class she gave us free time to draw whatever we wanted. I was big on horses then, though I'd never ridden one, and some of the guys liked to draw Nikes or basketball players soaring toward the rim. I had sketched in a light outline of a palomino when Ms. Omber leaned over to inspect. She put her tan hand next to my off-white paper and I could smell the bracing ocean breeze of her perfume. "Always remember Van Gogh's rule," she said, "lightest lights against darkest darks." I nodded, and trying to please her, changed my palomino to a pinto with dark spots.

After class I arrived at the locker before Arika did, and I saw some tapes that hadn't been there earlier, stacked on her shelf. I picked them up to read the labels: Too $hort, NWA, Public Enemy. I flipped a tape over to read the names of the songs and Arika came up behind me.

"Oh sorry," I said, jumping to put them back where I found them. "I was just—"

"Do you want to borrow them?" she asked. "You can take them home and dub them if you want."

"Really?" My voice practically squeaked. "That'd be great. When do you need them back?" I wondered if my mom would drive me to get some blank tapes that afternoon.

"Whenever." She threw me a half smile.

At home I carried the tapes up to my bedroom and closed the door. I drew as I listened to the music, which wasn't like anything I'd ever heard on the radio. It was angry and loud, with beats that made me tap my pencil against the sketchpad. I recognized some of the songs from the hallways and locker room at school, but it felt like a secret that I had discovered, music so full of filthy words, sex, and gunshots that no parent would hear it as anything but noise. I stayed up late dubbing them. Arika had written her address and phone number under the list of songs on *Fear of a Black Planet*, and I copied the information down. I packed the tapes into my backpack along with a bag of my mom's oatmeal pecan cookies to thank Arika.

The next day, though, whenever I saw Arika she was surrounded by friends, fuming, having angry conversations about some guy. "I know he *didn't*," she'd kept saying as I eavesdropped for more details.

When I walked in the art room, Ms. Omber was playing loud funk with blaring horns, "So I can't hear y'all bitchin," as she put it. Most the time Ms. Omber would be cooing, complimenting everything that came out of our pencils and offering help. But some days she was angry, and the wrinkles she'd amassed from cigarettes and too much sun would come out hard. She would yell when we did anything but sit in our seats, shut up and draw.

Ms. Omber turned down the radio to start us on an assignment, then cranked it again. Darnell shouted, "James Brown is tired!"

"Public Enemy doesn't think so," Ms. Omber said. She played a song that had a siren screaming through it, then said, "After class go get your Walkman and listen to *It Takes A Nation of Millions* again." She rapped a knuckle on Darnell's table. "Real art is never tired."

In the middle of class, Arika tried to sneak into the art supply room while Ms. Omber was assisting a special-ed kid with his project.

"Can I help you?" Ms. Omber asked.

"I need a new piece of paper," Arika said, with her hand on the door. "I already messed up once."

"Then you'll have to make art out of what you've got."

Arika wheeled around, muttering under her breath.

"You can leave," Ms. Omber said, and Arika stomped out of class, rolling her eyes and griping. I saw more dramatic exits at school every day than I did on the TV and had even heard rumors that an eighth grader had been suspended for beating a teacher unconscious, but Ms. Omber's class was a sort of harbor that usually no one wanted to be banished from.

Ms. Omber turned down the blaring funk. "You really can make art out of stuff other people would just throw away," she said. "I do it all the time."

"Can we see?" I asked.

She looked at me, as if surprised I'd spoken at last. "I don't see why not," she said.

Ms. Omber went into the supply room and came out with a few canvases. Everyone crowded around her desk, jostling each other for a better view. I squeezed in front, refusing to yield my space Darnell, who was jabbing me in the ribs with an elbow.

"I get most of my inspiration from Jamaica," she said, holding up a painting.

"You've never been to Jamaica," Darnell said, meaning it as a challenge. But it came out sounding like a wish that no one had experienced more than he had.

"Have too," she said. "I go all the time. I save up my money until I've got enough to go to Jamaica, then I stay there as long as it lasts."

I'd never heard of this kind of rootless behavior in any adult I knew, but back then it sounded like the whole point of being grown, so you could do whatever you wanted and no one could say anything about it.

Her collages were scenes of island life that lacked the glamour we expected of the tropics. Bits of corrugated cardboard, split open to reveal the wavy center, posed as the tin roofs of the shacks in shantytowns. She constructed entire streets with ripped paper figures, and then covered everything with color so it became a textured painting, bright and crowded with life. I asked about the materials so I could practice the technique at home. "That's just from an old box I found in the alley," she told me.

"How much people pay you for these?" Darnell asked.

"That's for me to know," Ms. Omber said. "But it don't pay the rent, if that's what you're thinking."

The key to her collages was that nothing looked too precise—she tore the shapes to the edge of perfection but held back, never making them fussily exact. That seemed to be the way to get along at school, too. Don't pull your pants too high and cinch them to your waist like you were worried about anyone ever trying to get in them, or throw your arm up in the air to answer a teacher too quick or reveal a desperate cache of information when people asked you a simple question.

On the way out of class, I checked the masterpiece board to see if any of my pictures had made it up. One of Reggie's over-muscled basketball men claimed the corner, and there was a bubble letter collage by Arika, and some colorful designs by the special-ed kids. There was a dark, storm-like picture by Tracy Cohen, whose dad had died of skin cancer the year before. When I didn't see one of mine, I tried to console myself with the thought that she taught six classes and had to make room for everyone. Still, it burned me that as hard as I worked, Ms. Omber didn't seem to think I was good.

Arika was leaning against our locker after the bell rang, staring straight ahead, pretending not to see me, holding her face in a tough expression that looked on the verge of cracking.

I wondered why she hadn't gone home after Ms. Omber sent her out. It was almost as though she expected the teacher to come after her. "Ms. Omber acts so crazy sometimes," I said, trying to commiserate, even though our teacher's moods didn't bother me.

Arika glanced at me. "Probably because she's hiding her big weed stash back in that room." She shifted over so I could open the locker.

Others had accused Ms. Omber of drug use, but even if she were a pothead, I'd still have worshipped her. What I cared about was that she was the first art teacher who treated us like artists in training. Still, this was the longest conversation I'd had with Arika and I tried to keep it going. "It's like Ms. Omber is trans," I began, "except she feels she's really Black." It was quite possibly the stupidest thing I'd ever said.

Arika looked at me, serious. "You mean, like, she's transblack?" She cracked up, repeating the word, *transblack* between gasps. "Y'all are too funny," she said, as if I'd invented the term.

I dug through my backpack so I wouldn't have to look at her as she kept laughing. "Here are the tapes back," I said, holding them out. "Thanks." I decided to eat the cookies myself on the bus ride home.

The next day I worked up the nerve to ask Ms. Omber about the masterpiece board. I thought maybe she'd just forgotten to put one of mine up. "How do you pick what goes up there?" I asked.

She leaned down so that her face was right near mine. "It's people's best work. The best they can do."

I'd done plenty of good drawings, and my ears grew hot from the injustice of it, but I nodded and picked up my pencil again. As I was drawing, Darnell walked by and tapped me on the shoulder, saying, "Hey, transblackula."

"Shut up," I said.

He walked off, making *bla bla bla* vampire sounds and flapping his arms like wings.

The first snow came in mid-October, and the hot-water radiators hissed on in the drafty hallways. Ms. Omber wore a bulky sweater that hung down past her butt, and she walked around hugging herself and rubbing her arms with her hands for warmth.

"Wish I was in Jamaica today," she said as we drew.

While the snow fell outside and the gloomy light filtered in through the windows, she showed us some of her Jamaica photographs, the turquoise ocean and yellow sand matching our vague ideas of islands and the sea. I tried to imagine what the ocean would smell like, what it would sound like. But she mostly photographed people or junk, streets full of ramshackle houses and people with snaggletoothed smiles, barefoot, wearing mismatched clothing. The same man turned up in the pictures repeatedly. The top of his brown head was bald and he had a curly beard with a touch of silver in it. His eyes were mirthful, the bottom lid arched. When Arika asked about him, Ms. Omber said, "Mind your own."

I decided that this Jamaican man had broken Ms. Omber's heart and kept on breaking it, even though I didn't have any experience with those concerns outside of frequent, doomed crushes. Maybe there was a man who kept drawing her back and pushing her away, and that's why she was cranky some days. This story fit with the image of the romantic artist I'd painted for Ms. Omber in my mind.

Ms. Omber announced that we were going to learn how to draw people. She passed around a picture of a woman's face that an art magazine had dissected. Nobody recognized her, but Ms. Omber said, "It's Farrah Fawcett, an actress from back in the day, and some said she was the most beautiful woman in the world."

"Like who?" shouted Darnell. "She looks goofy."

"Men who like blondes," Ms. Omber said. "Look, I didn't pick the person the magazine decided to feature. But if you check the measurements, everything's wrong. Her eyes are two different sizes and her mouth isn't the same on both sides. There's no such thing as a perfect face, so don't be afraid. If you mess up a little, it probably looks more natural anyhow."

She drew the outline of the face, sketching different shapes on the chalkboard, some oval, some round, some ending in a point like a heart. Then she moved onto eyes, sketching an almond shape on the chalkboard. She added the tear duct, saying, "It has to have that little muscle at the corner or it'll pop out." She drew the circle of the iris, put a pupil in the center, started to shade the iris in, then stopped. "You always have to leave a little light in it," she said. "I know that because I've seen a dead man's eyes." The boys in the back of the room came back like a chorus: *Damn!*

She put down her chalk. "I was walking my dog and he started barking and running up toward this thing on the top of a hill," she said. "I followed to see what it was. A dead man was on his back, eyes open, staring at the sky. Those eyes were flat and dull. There was nothing in them, no light. Looking at them made me stop breathing for a second." She stared off toward the frosted windows. Then she snapped out of her trance and added, "So when you draw eyes, leave a fleck of light instead of coloring in the iris completely—that makes them come alive."

"I've seen a dead man too," Reggie said quietly.

Ms. Omber looked at him, shaking her head softly. "I know you have, baby."

We waited for more, realized that was all she had to say on the subject, then attempted to draw eyes, leaving a tiny box or bubble unshaded in the irises. It was a Friday afternoon, and everyone around me chattered about what they were going to do that weekend.

It took the bus over an hour to get us home in the snow. When I walked in the door, I forced myself to go to the phone and dial Arika's number.

"Hi," I said when someone answered. "Is Arika there?"

"That's me."

"Hey, it's Emily."

"Emily from school Emily?" She sounded incredulous.

"Yeah. Look," I plunged on rather than explaining how I got her number, "I was wondering if you copied down the science homework?"

"Hang on a minute." I heard her rummaging through a bag. "Read chapter six and do the questions at the end."

"Odds or evens?"

"Both, I think."

"The odd ones are answered in the back."

"Yeah." She chuckled. "I know."

I took a deep breath. "Hey, do you want to see a movie sometime? Everybody says that *House Party* is good. It's playing at the cheapo place near me."

She didn't say anything for a second. "I don't know. Where do you live?"

"In the south. By Rosamond Park."

"Never heard of it."

"I could probably get a ride to a place near where you live—by school, right?"

"Yeah, but the closest theater is downtown. I don't have a ride though. My mom works weekends."

"Oh," I said, feeling stupid. "Well, I guess I'll see you Monday then."

"Sure."

After I hung up I pressed the receiver to my forehead until it left a dent. I should have offered to have my mom pick her up. But that was the one time I'd ever try that.

The next Monday, Ms. Omber told us to partner up and draw each other. Arika chose Keisha, the girl she always sat with. Tracy

Cohen took up with Roland, a blond headbanger in an "Alcoholica: Drink 'em All" T-shirt. Even Reggie found a partner, a guy who liked the Air Jordan pictures he drew and wanted a good portrait to give to his mother. Everyone else started drawing as I sat alone.

Eventually Ms. Omber came over and asked, "Don't you have a partner?" I shook my head. "Well you should speak up." She sat down next to me and stared at my face. When I didn't pick up my pencil she said, "Go ahead, start drawing me." I didn't know what was more terrifying, seeing how I would appear in her drawing or trying to capture her in mine.

My hands sweated on my eraser and pencil as I tried to begin. Ms. Omber was a real artist, and her picture might show me as I was. I searched for the lines in Ms. Omber's face, some clear angle to start with. These shapes, the triangles and circles that formed the cheeks and chin and brow, were harder to determine on a live person than on a picture of one. I started with her eyes, because whenever I began with an outline of the face I always ended up positioning the features incorrectly, too high or low or bunched together and the people ended up looking like pigs or aliens. Ms. Omber must have been in her thirties, but there were so many lines around her eyes it was impossible to catch them all. I drew some of them, and then began to make out the geometry of her nose, the planes of her forehead, the curve of her lips. She didn't look right with her skin the color of the paper so I shaded it and worked hard to capture the fuzzy texture of her dreads. After a while, staring at her didn't make me any more uncomfortable than looking at the horses in my picture books. I was breathing deeply and didn't notice the time, squeezing the warm kneaded-gum eraser in my left hand, my right hand picking up a black smudge along the edge and a pencil dent on my middle finger as I worked.

The other students began to mill around us, standing over her and looking up from her drawing to my face. I'd forgotten about Ms. Omber's portrait of me while I was drawing, but now the fear of it lay heavy on my stomach. I felt so awkward all the time, I didn't understand how the Black girls could be so comfortable with themselves, boastful of their curves, styling and adorning their hair until it gleamed like plumage. In our locker, Arika's bra would reappear on occasion. I was too shy to ask her if it was a spare, or if she was just taking a breather from it, or what.

"How do you do that, Ms. Omber?" they asked. Apparently, she had me cold. "Practice, that's all." My eyes began to fill, and I didn't want to cry in front of everyone so I tried to hold back.

Arika came around and looked at my drawing. "Hey, that's good. Darnell, come look at this." He came over, and some of his buddies did too. "That's Miss O all right. That's her hair." He ran his fingers over a dred, smudging the pencil a little. "You draw all the time or something?" I realized he was asking me a question and I nodded, afraid that if I spoke my voice would crack.

"You're a good drawer," Arika declared.

It felt great to hear this. Then the bell rang and the crowd dispersed and I was left there sitting in my chair, trying to gather my stuff so I wouldn't miss the bus.

"You want this?" Ms. Omber asked, holding out her drawing of me. I still couldn't look at it.

"No thanks," I said.

She pursed her lips. "Sure you do. Take this home, give it to your mama." She handed it to me. "She'll want it."

I took the drawing from her and jogged down the stairs with my backpack thumping and climbed onto the bus just before it pulled away. I sat in the first empty seat and caught my breath, afraid to flip over the paper that I held in my hand. Finally, after we'd pulled out and passed the former crack house that had been painted pink and turned into a community day care, then covered again with gang graffiti—*crip cuzz, slob killer*—I looked at it. There were my big lips and thick eyebrows. Were they really that big? Ms. Omber had been honest. Each part alone seemed strange, but when I held it back and saw the whole face it looked all right. It was the face of a shy person, a hesitant person, someone who wouldn't let too much of what she felt show. I thought of Arika, her anti–poker face, her eyebrows always forming the punctuation to her moods. I stared at my face the whole way home, looking from the paper to my reflection in the bus window, trying to see myself as beautiful, then ran up to my room and hid the picture in my sketchbook.

The next day I walked into class and saw my drawing of Ms. Omber hanging in the middle of the masterpiece board. I stopped and breathed in the room's scent of chalk dust, pencil shavings, and tempura paint. I took a step back to admire it. The features grew indistinct when I stood too far away. I hadn't shaded the shadows dark enough. But I felt proud to have made the board and kept glancing back during class to see if any of the other kids were looking at my drawing.

Winter hit hard that year, and snow piled up along the streets, white for a fleeting moment before it was splattered with slush. The city always managed to clear the roads in time to ship us to school, even if it took hours. Ms. Omber developed a terrible cough. It rattled in her chest and set her to spasms. When a coughing fit ended, she would lose her train of thought and forget to finish the instructions she was giving us. This made the guys in the back snicker and speculate about her drug use. Arika, who bore a grudge like a mafia don, had been sharing her pot theory with everyone. "I mean, who goes to Jamaica and doesn't smoke the ganja?" she'd ask anyone who'd listen. To me Ms. Omber just seemed like a person who wasn't built for the cold, who was meant for warmer places but had become stuck here somehow.

I'd tried a few times to defend Ms. Omber, but I was getting tired of it. She never spent as much time helping me as she did the others, never called me "baby." I wanted to be an artist and I wanted Ms. Omber to tell me that I was one, but she never did.

The first week in December, there was a winter social in the gym during the last two periods of class. They had the dances during the school day, I figured, because none of the bused kids' parents would allow them to return to the school's neighborhood after dark. The gym looked the same as usual, black metal bars over the windows and sneaker streaks on the old wood floor. Someone had put up a few construction paper snowflakes on one wall, and there was a boombox in the corner, playing Salt-N-Pepa, En Vogue, and Bell Biv Devoe. Arika was with a group of girls dancing to the music. It looked like they'd memorized the exact moves from the videos, and they missed no beats. I went over to the table where the science teacher was pouring glasses of punch. Tracy Cohen caught up with me, and I handed her a cup. We leaned against the wall together, to watch the other kids have fun. "This is lame," she said, and I clinked my plastic cup against hers.

The boombox played a slow tune and the dancers cleared the floor. The guys hung in clumps around the perimeter of the gym, some of them dribbling basketballs, sullen because the teacher said they couldn't hoop during the dance. Roland came over to talk to Tracy, and I inched away down the wall.

Arika walked up and leaned against the wall next to me. She wiped the back of her hand across her forehead. "I am sweating!"

She laughed and grabbed my hand. "Hey, come over with me to get some punch."

I followed, half afraid she was going to make me try to dance or repeat the transblack comment to her friends or something. She grabbed some punch and tossed it back.

Across from the punch keg, a long piece of butcher paper was stretched across the wall, and kids were drawing a mural on it with the scented magic markers that everybody loved. "Let's check that out," Arika said.

We ran into Keisha on the way across the gym. "Hey this is Emily, my locker partner," she said.

"Oh hey," Keisha said, "from art class, right? You drew that sweet picture of Ms. O."

I nodded, feeling giddy. It seemed that talent was a key that opened people to you, so they didn't care about any of your other details for as long as you could do what you could do.

"Why don't you do a picture of me and Keisha up on the wall?" Arika said.

"Okay." We went to the mural and found an empty place. I took up one of the brown markers that smelled like cinnamon and started working on their faces, even though it was too dark for Arika's skin. I drew their hair with the licorice-scented black marker. When I was done, it didn't look exactly like them, but it did look like real people, and Keisha and Arika were pleased. They signed their names in mango-scented turquoise underneath, both of them in an elaborate cursive with a star over the i's in their names. Arika handed me the pen. "You sign, too." I couldn't help smiling as I did.

The day after the social, a substitute teacher sat at Ms. Omber's desk. We all laughed while this little white man in a sweater vest with round glasses read down the grade book as he called roll, mispronouncing every third name. The guys in the back seized on this and tormented each other. Darnell yelled at ShaQuan, "Hey, SHACK-wan, use the force!"

The sub looked up. "Ms. Omber told me that you all have projects to be working on, so why don't you get right to it."

"Yes, why don't we," Arika said in a white person accent, and everybody sniggered.

I started drawing like always, but then I heard the whispers. The supply room door was ajar. Boys were daring each other to go back there, saying, "Naw, you do it," back and forth. "Somebody's gotta do it," Arika said. "A chance like this don't come around twice."

I turned to face them. "I'll do it," I said, "if you distract the teacher."

My portrait of Ms. Omber was my only drawing to appear on the masterpiece board in months. "You've got to loosen up, Emily," she'd tell me, when I turned in another technically precise drawing of a person or animal. When she said that, I'd dig my fingernails into my palms. I'd seen what happened to people at that school who loosened up, like the fourteen-year-old mom who had brought her baby in to visit. The mother had sucked on the baby's pacifier while Ms. Omber fussed over the infant.

Darnell planned the diversion. He went to the back of the room and looked outside. "Hey, Mister Teacher," he said. "There's a trashcan in the hallway on fire." The teacher rushed out. I slipped into the supply room.

I had to blink to acclimate my sight in the dark room. Shelves were filled with different colors and sizes of paper, glue, scissors, pencils, and markers. I couldn't walk out there and tell them that was all I'd seen, so I kept looking. On the back wall her paintings hung, each of them awash in aquamarine, each set in the same shanty town neighborhood, and hung side by side in such a way that it seemed she was trying to recreate an entire street from memory. It was beautiful, even though the people and buildings it depicted were shabby. They didn't have any features on their faces, but the shape of their bodies expressed what they were feeling, stooped or proud, plump or famine skinny. And the colors she used for their skin were all shades of brown.

I looked in the drawers of the desk, hoping to find something interesting. The first drawer held rubber bands and paper clips in a tangle. The next one was stuffed with pictures, some of them that she'd shown us. The pictures of the man were the first I saw. He was laughing in some, serious in others, usually half dressed in white linen shirts, as if he were overheated. One picture was curled as if it had been wet, and a few had paint fingerprints in the corners. There was one photo I hadn't seen before, with Ms. Omber next to the man on the beach. She wore an orange bikini top and a white sarong. He had his arm around her waist and his lips on her cheek. She faced the camera and laughed.

I could take it, I thought, draw it, and then turn the photo and the drawing in anonymously. It would be my masterpiece. She'd put it on the board and say that she'd forgive whoever had done the drawing because they had done it so well, and I'd raise my hand to claim it, suddenly worthy of her attention.

I heard the sub shout, "Who's in there?" My heartbeat skittered but I still managed to think. I slipped the photo into the pocket of my jeans and snatched a piece of paper on the way out. Sweat was rolling down the sub's forehead and it had only been five minutes since the beginning of class. Even I had power over him. "I messed up," I told him. "So I took a new piece of paper."

"Well, ask first next time."

"Ms. Omber lets us get it ourselves," I said, and everyone snickered.

The sub's eyes darted from one kid to the next. "Everyone sit in your seat right now and draw."

I did as he said, but everybody gathered around me.

"So what'd you see?" Arika asked. "A big old stash?"

"No," I said, and the sly smiles fell off everyone's faces, but they didn't turn to walk back to their seats. They were waiting for me to say more. I could have showed them the picture, but I was keeping it for myself. Still, I wanted to be a part of their fun, their gossip, their easy banter. I wanted to loosen up. "I saw a crack pipe," I said.

Darnell hooted.

"For real?" Arika said.

I nodded. I don't know if they believed me or not, but they all started laughing, saying *I knew it! I told you she was hitting that rock!* I felt good, a part of the crowd, but only for a moment, and then the bell rang and they went their way and I went mine, to snag a lonely seat on the cross-town bus.

When Ms. Omber came back the next week, she was trying to demonstrate how to draw hands, but the boys at the back of the room kept laughing until she yelled, "What the fuck is so funny?" They just raised their eyes toward the ceiling like angels to God and wouldn't answer. I felt a pang of regret then and turned toward her. I wanted to return the photo and apologize. Even if she didn't like me, I was sorry I'd lied about her. She said, "What are you looking at?" and threw down her chalk. She stormed into the supply room, coughing, slamming the door behind her. For once, everyone was quiet.

I started the drawing of Ms. Omber and her boyfriend a few times, but couldn't get the details right—the hands, the eyes. I couldn't make out the man's features well enough where they were darker because of the shadow Ms. Omber cast on his face. I procrastinated about it until school let out for winter break, and the next semester I walked into the art room and found a new teacher there, a young woman with wide blue eyes, sitting on the edge of Ms. Omber's desk.

"Did Ms. Omber go to Jamaica?" I demanded.

She laughed, smoothing her hands over her long denim skirt. "You're the fifth student to ask me that today."

Casa del Rey

The dead man's condo sat empty for a year before Venita moved in. We'd called the dead man "Portrait in Courage" because of the way he used to jog daily on the bike path nearby, despite the awkward hitch to his gait. He'd moved slower than the pace at which most people walked, but we could tell by the way he pumped his arms that he thought of it as running. "Nothing we have to do is that difficult," I'd tell my husband, Jamie.

We lived in Casa del Rey, a condo complex built in 1979 that was patterned in a faux-Southwestern style, with flat roofs, peach stucco, cheap tile, and wrought iron accents. Until we bought the condo, college students had rented it, and it showed: candle wax trails down the walls, rotted floorboards in the bathroom, dark streaks that looked like bicycle tracks on the ceiling. At some point, climbers had rented it and there were handholds bolted into the walls in places you'd think only Spider-Man could reach.

The day I met Venita, I was almost three months pregnant and hauling grocery bags from my car when a mangled Impala drove up, bashed in on every side, its panels bulging, trim sagging, and mysterious clumps of wires snaking free. The sunroof was smashed in, as though something round and heavy had crushed it. Its headlights dangled, and an orange strap held the front bumper in place. Inside, the car was stuffed with bags, trash, and balled-up clothes, the distance from front seat to back window spanned by a rolled rattan shade and a single crutch.

A woman shambled out of the Impala, her long stringy hair piled on top of her head, her glasses magnifying her eyes, which were all pupil. She wore sweatpants that sagged in the butt, one leg hitched higher than the other. "Do you live here?" she demanded.

I hesitated. "Yes," I admitted, never able to think of an honest way out of those inescapable opening lines of salespeople and the deranged.

"I'm Venita," she said, extending her hand.

"Kari," I said, shaking it.

"I'm considering buying the corner unit." She nodded toward Portrait in Courage's condo, "but the parking space assigned to it is too far away. Would you be willing to trade your space?"

The crutch made me waver, but then I remembered the baby. "I don't think so. We like our space."

"Do you know who owns these cars?" She gestured at the vehicles in the other nearby spaces.

I shook my head. She looked like if you so much as told her the time she'd ask you to jumpstart her car next.

I heaved some bags from the trunk and carried them toward my condo. We had been concerned about how long it was taking the empty place to sell, but I'd rather live next to Portrait in Courage's mellow ghost than have this specimen for a neighbor.

Leaves crunched underfoot behind me. "I'll be getting knee surgery in the spring," Venita said, following me down the sidewalk. "You really won't consider trading your space?"

"I'm having a baby," I blurted. "I'll need to park close to our house." Something about this woman made me feel I was fighting for control of the space even though it was already mine.

"Oh," she said. "When?"

Her question felt invasive, but I'd brought us down this road. "In April." I thought about that crazy woman in New Mexico who'd cut a pregnant lady's stomach open with her car keys to get at the baby inside. I'd earned my black belt in Tae Kwon Do when I was thirteen, and I probably still remembered enough to collapse a larynx with the side of my hand. I liked my chances as a pregnant lady in a balls-out scrap. "Why don't you call Bruce, the property manager," I suggested, "and see if anybody will trade."

"I already did."

"Well, good luck with that." I loaded my arms with too many grocery sacks so I wouldn't have to make a second trip and pulled the door closed behind me.

I didn't mention the conversation to Jamie, but he found out about it at the next homeowner's association board meeting. He came home and went straight to the refrigerator for a beer.

"Apparently this Venita woman is calling Bruce twelve times a day," he said. "She wants a parking space, she wants to knock down a wall so that she can have a window on the south side, she wants to install an air conditioning unit that's against the regulations. And Bruce comes up to me and says, *I hear you're in the family way* and does this lewd wink. He made it sound like having a baby is something dirty."

"Our baby is clean," I said. "It's the cleanest thing we've ever done."

"Why did you tell her that you're pregnant?" He flipped off the top of his beer with a bottle opener and let the cap fall to the ground. "We haven't even told our friends yet."

I looked at the green bottle cap on the floor and thought of the choking risk it posed. "I just wanted her to stop asking for our parking spot."

"I don't want our baby playing with any of the kids in Caca del Rey," Jaime said, chopping the air with his hand. "The kids here are unsavory."

There were barely any kids around the complex except for a roving band of twelve-year-old boys who appeared intermittently, probably for court-ordered visitations with a parent. They chucked rocks and trash around the grounds, dropped their cigarette butts everywhere, and hung out at the pathetic kidney-shaped swimming pool, leering like teens in '50s motorcycle movies. I thought about our baby going into a neighbor's condo to play and pictured a haze of cigarette smoke, dark curtains over the windows, and a slatternly mother with her breast half exposed in a silk kimono at midday. Jamie was right—Caca del Rey was no place to raise a child, but I didn't know how we'd manage to move.

At first we were happy in the condo, the best place within Boulder that we could afford. Two different trailer parks surrounded Casa del Rey, each owned by the city of Boulder to maintain a few pockets of affordable housing. There was an irrigation ditch behind our unit that we thought of as a stream, flanked by a wetland project that the city council was tending, mounting bird censuses and blasting with wildflower seeds through a sort of gun. The trailer park on the other side of the ditch was a tight community, populated by hippies and single mothers with passels of children who congregated at a trampoline. In summer we'd sit out on the porch, watching the sun set behind the Flatirons, and listen to the joyful shouts of the bouncing children until dusk when the hummingbirds left and the bats came out, serrated wings beating jagged paths through the sky.

We'd talk about painting over the bicycle streaks someday, replacing the stained carpet that always reminded me of the time at a college party I'd seen a dog with worms drag his itching butt across the floor.

Usually on summer evenings, Sally, our neighbor to the east, would come out onto her porch and grill a portobello mushroom.

"It's a beautiful day," she'd say with feeling, as she did every evening, a lobotomized look in her eyes. "Yeah, it sure is," one of us would answer. Like many women in Boulder, Sally didn't use makeup, let her hair go gray, and wore the sort of utilitarian moisture-wicking khaki pants with abundant pockets that were sold in travel stores. We liked Sally. She reminded us of the old Boulder, before sleek coastal women with standing hair appointments had invaded.

Our neighbor to the west was another single woman, Dolores, who housed a rotating group of roommates and was in the middle of foreclosure procedures because she hadn't paid the homeowner's association dues in two years. Jamie had joined the HOA board to press for the repair of a persistent roof leak, and sitting on the board gave him an unfortunate front-row view into the gaping maw of other people's financial troubles. Dolores tried to throw off the process servers who came to tape notices to her door by installing incorrect brass address numbers outside her unit.

The dead neighbor had lived on the other side of Dolores. One day we noticed a pile of newspapers accumulating outside his door, each in its orange plastic bag. As the pile grew, we told ourselves that he'd gone on vacation and forgotten to stop delivery.

After ten days of newspapers, an ambulance and three police cars came. I watched out the window as a man and woman talked to a compact policewoman. The ambulance didn't speed away with its siren blaring. It just drove off after a while, slowly navigating over the two yellow speed bumps in the parking lot.

A few days later, we saw the same couple loading things into a truck. The man told us he was a friend of Richard, which turned out to be Portrait in Courage's name, and that he had no family in state, so they were clearing out his stuff as best they could. "He had been dead a couple of days before they found him," he said.

We nodded, thinking, *More than a couple of days.*

"Was he sick?" I asked. Finally, we would learn the nature of Portrait in Courage's mysterious ailment that caused him such difficulty when he ran.

"They suspect it was a heart attack," the man said. "The coroner said that Richard had high blood pressure and was being treated for it."

"How old was he?" Jamie asked. His father had died of a heart attack. It was a pet peeve of his when obituaries omitted either the age or the cause of death.

"Only fifty-nine."

Later that night when neither of us could sleep, I asked Jamie, "Could we have saved him?"

"He'd have been long dead."

"I guess we couldn't have known the first day he didn't pick up his paper."

"Well, there's one less newspaper subscriber in the world now."

Portrait in Courage's friends returned for months, mucking out his condo. The piles out front would shift as they worked, and I learned about Richard through them. He'd owned a pair of every type of ski—downhill, skate, telemark, classic. I wished I'd spoken with him about skiing, asked him for tips on his favorite trails. One day there was a stack of fourteen orange and brown Nike boxes, and I thought, *Richard was the sort of guy who kept his shoes in their original boxes.*

Eventually his friends stopped coming around and a realtor began to show people Richard's condo, but for a year no one bought it, perhaps because they could sense that a man had spent the last days of his lonely life there, or perhaps because of the vibe of the entire condo complex, full of divorcées, widowers, and renters who'd lost homes.

Life in the surrounding trailer parks seemed more vivid. We'd walk through the trailer park to the west on a summer night and think we were in some colorful Guatemalan town, all the kids riding their bicycles out in the street, squealing, chattering in Spanish, their parents out on their porches under strings of Christmas lights, gabbing with the neighbors, all the radios down the strip tuned to La Tricolor 96.5, the ice-cream man playing his tinny, maniacal song over and over while the kids ran up to him, their flip-flops skidding on the pavement, a paletera wheeling his cart into the chaos, hawking mango and pineapple fruit-pops. Then we'd turn the corner and no one would be outside.

Until Venita moved in, Casa del Rey was quiet. The only signs of activity came from the college renters, such as the pair of grim longhairs who blasted Black Sabbath into the night, and a young woman who liked loud sex. We could hear her moaning for extended periods at any hour of the day or night. When I was out front, tending my two-foot patch of petunias, I'd see her get out of her car, her long hair swinging like she was starring in a shampoo commercial, and I'd think, *There she goes. Off to have some ecstatic sex.*

"Nutjob's loan has been approved," Jamie announced one evening when he returned from a three-hour HOA meeting. He went straight for the Scotch. "I want to get out of here."

"Agreed." I was five months pregnant and my job as a database administrator for an organic dog food company was going nowhere. I wanted to stay home and raise the baby by hand, free range, like in the olden days, but we didn't know if we could afford it.

"We could live in one of the trailer parks," he suggested. "Take your pick, Hippieland or Little Guatemala."

"A trailer is a step down from a condo," I said. "Isn't it?" I pictured our kid, barefoot in sackcloth with a dustbowl face.

"I'm not so sure anymore," Jamie said. "At least there are families with happy kids in the trailer parks."

I nodded. "You never see the boys around here smile."

"They're too busy smoking," Jaime said. "We might have to both keep working so we can get out of here."

"But what good is a new house if no one's home?"

The next day I returned from work, eager to deflate my swollen feet by hoisting them up on the couch. But Venita's Impala was parked in my spot. Her move-in day was a week off, and she was already omnipresent. Normally I hesitated to call the tow-truck company listed on the reserved parking signs throughout the lot, and instead knocked on neighbors' doors and consulted with Sally and Dolores until I could find the car's owner, but I was exhausted. I called the towing company, and then parked my car near the 7-Eleven down the block, fuming about my aching feet and back as I trudged home. I hoped Venita would come out when the tow truck arrived. I watched through the kitchen window as the driver puzzled over where to safely attach his cable. I expected parts of the Impala to fall off as he dragged it over the speed bumps, but it held together.

The Impala returned a few days later, occupying the no-parking zone behind my car as Venita moved in, making runs to haul her crap from wherever she'd kept it before. Jamie scowled out through our kitchen window. "That can't be legal to drive," he said. "I mean, what the hell happened to the sunroof?"

"Her ex was a bowler?" I suggested.

"Portrait in Courage was uplifting," he said. "This new neighbor is the opposite of that."

"Downlifting?"

"Or down dragging. She'll drag us all down with her if we're not careful." Jamie shut the blinds. "More birds will probably come to shit on our car now."

Venita was high-impact, her car dropping trash as it farted into view, advertising circulars escaping as she rummaged and blowing around like tumbleweeds in the parking lot. As she settled in, sketchy workmen started driving up in unmarked white vans, walking in and out of her condo and playing stupid morning drive-time radio shows loud enough for everyone to hear. Shirtless men, bronze in midwinter, came every week to deliver her bottled water. She'd started a compost pile, which she tended poorly, and many nights we'd awaken to the almost-human screams of raccoons squabbling over Venita's eggshells and fish bones. She had so much stuff her condo couldn't contain it, and it belched out onto her porch and into the collective area in front of the condos, where a chipped plaster statue of Buddha and one of the Virgin Mary stared each other down. Venita's way of hedging her bets.

The doctor put me on bed rest two weeks before my due date because of my high blood pressure. The condition made me feel a kinship with Richard, and I wondered if he'd felt this way, light-headed and sleepy. I tried to read parenting books, but what I mostly did was nap after sleepless nights filled with the raccoons' murderous screams and watch Venita's activity from the window in the nursery that looked out on the parking lot. Jamie had headed up the HOA's offensive on the illegal compost pile, drafting letters with increasingly terse wording, threatening fines, but so far the raccoon haven remained. I'd called the tow truck on Venita four more times. Twice Venita arrived to intervene, and twice the wrecker dragged the forlorn Impala away backward over the speed bumps. Venita's assigned spot was only thirty yards away, but my space, open all day while I was at work, was too tempting for her. I suspected all the drama with Venita and the tow truck had caused my blood pressure problems. At least now that I was on bed rest, our car could guard our spot except when I needed to leave for doctor's appointments.

The baby squirmed inside me after midnight, fluttering her toes, climbing my ribs, sometimes ramming so hard against me that a softball-sized bulge would press out, and I couldn't sleep; all I could do was think about Venita. I'd observe her activity during the day and describe it to Jamie the minute he came home. "Did you see she's got a handicapped tag on her rearview mirror now?" I asked him. She wore a brace and hobbled around, making a big production out of it, unlike Richard, who'd tried to hide his limp. "She doesn't deserve to live in Portrait in Courage's condo."

One day I checked to make sure Venita wasn't in the parking lot, and then went to get the mail, enjoying the novelty of the short walk. When I returned, Venita was out rummaging through her car. I felt uneasy as I passed her. Venita looked right at me, but I pretended not to notice. She seemed just crazy enough to enact some kind of revenge on me for all the towing.

A few minutes later, the doorbell rang. I considered not answering it, but my curiosity got the better of me. It was lonely waiting at home for the baby, waiting to find out what the pain would be like. There was a time every afternoon when the baby always went dead still for too long, and I'd press a music box against my skin and worry as I tried to get her to respond.

When I opened the door, Venita was standing there with a tense, expectant look. Maybe she was going to tell me off for towing her car.

"I don't think I've met you," she said. "I'm new, I'm Venita."

"We've met," I said, and left it at that, the way I imagined John Wayne would've. She must have known I'd called the tow truck on her car. Was she pretending not to know me because she wanted something, or was she really that spacey?

"I'm locked out of my place," she said in the pathetic tone she probably used all the time, with doctors, cops, the lady behind the counter at the DMV. "I thought I had a spare key in my car, but I've been looking for it and I can't find it. My phone is inside my condo."

"Do you want to borrow my phone to call a locksmith?"

"Too expensive," she said. "I wanted to call Bruce."

I admitted her into the house and brought her the phone, wondering what she was thinking Bruce could do for her.

"Do you have a ladder?" she asked me after Bruce shot her down. "I left the balcony door on the second floor unlocked, so if I could just get up there—"

I shook my head. "No. No ladders." I opened the door for her to leave.

"Could I use your bathroom?" She sounded like a five-year-old.

I wanted to kick her out, but I wasn't that John Wayne. "Upstairs," I said, jerking my thumb. *Three minutes, Pilgrim*, I thought.

She inspected our condo as she limped through it. "I wish I had a south-facing window," she said. The HOA had denied her permission to knock out a load-bearing wall. "This place is going to be pretty snug when the baby gets here," she said. "How will you all fit?"

"We'll manage."

After she left, I waddled over to the couch and tested my blood pressure, which was in the safe range. In a few minutes, the doorbell rang again. Of course Venita was there.

"I found a ladder," she said. There were bits of leaves in her hair. "Can you hold it steady while I climb?"

I'm nine months pregnant and supposed to be on bed rest, I thought. I wished I were wearing one of those obnoxious T-shirts to highlight the fact, *Under Construction,* with an arrow pointing down. Still, I felt guilty about having her car towed. The Impala couldn't have been worth the money she must have spent to spring it three times from the impound lot. Maybe if I held the ladder, she would set aside whatever homicidal plan she was concocting against me. And I was bored, deeply bored. So I followed her. She complimented me on the view that we had behind our condo, sounding like she wanted to claim it as her own. I grunted in response, my ankles tender and swollen from standing. She limped along in front of me, complaining of back pain. I didn't respond. I would not engage in a comparison of ailments with Venita.

There was a twenty-foot aluminum extension ladder leaning against her balcony. Tufts of spring snow rested in the corner of each step. She mounted the ladder and I took my position below, gripping the freezing metal. My hands turned pink, the knuckles white, and I worried about how I'd prevent my child from one day licking cold metal on a dare.

She climbed slowly and when she got to the top, she hesitated, holding onto the ladder and leaning forward to peer over the balcony's four-foot wall. "Oh boy," she said, then awkwardly vaulted herself over onto the upper deck. There was a thud and then a chain-reaction of commotion that sounded like she'd hit a bunch of pots and pans on the way down.

"You all right up there?" I asked.

She didn't respond.

"Hey, Venita?" I said to the silent balcony. For a few minutes I called her name. *Veh-neee-tah.* I was pretty sure climbing ladders was not allowed on bed rest. I chugged over to Dolores's place, the baby roiling inside of me, my stomach a concrete-filled basketball that pulled at my skin as it moved up and down. But Dolores and Sally were at work.

My face was flushed and I was short of breath. I didn't want to spike my blood pressure, so I went home. I picked up the telephone, trying to formulate a story for police. If something happened to Venita, surely they would talk to the neighbors and find out that I was always calling the tow truck on her. It would look like I had some kind of vendetta against her. I pictured a visit from Jamie and the baby through a pane of prison Plexiglass, the baby's little hand pressed against the window as she leaned in to taste the partition with her pink tongue. I replaced the phone in its cradle. I considered going to the 7-Eleven down the street to use the pay phone and call in an anonymous tip, but I wasn't supposed to walk that far. Hoping the police would pity me in my overripe state, I rang the non-emergency number. I spoke carefully to the dispatcher so I wouldn't be lying, "I think my neighbor fell from a ladder." I explained that she hadn't fallen to the ground, just onto her balcony, and they said they'd send someone to check on her.

Just after I reported Venita's accident, the obstetrician's office called to ask why I was fifteen minutes late for my appointment. I'd forgotten it the moment Venita appeared on my doorstep. My stomach tightened and pains from the ligaments stretching shot through my sides. The receptionist said they could still work me in, so I left and never saw if the ambulance arrived. As I drove off I thought of Portrait in Courage and hoped his condo hadn't doomed Venita to a similar fate.

I told Jamie about the whole fiasco when he came home from work.

"You're supposed to be on bed rest," Jamie said, his face stern as a father's. "Hauling ladders around and calling the cops doesn't sound like rest to me." He cupped his hands over my stomach and called to the baby, "Are you all right in there?"

"I didn't carry the ladder. And what should I have done? She's our neighbor."

"We didn't ask her to move in."

I pictured the baby at thirteen, scowling, telling me that she didn't ask to be born.

The next morning I rang Venita's doorbell and there was no answer. I looked through the spider-webbed cracks in the windows of her car to see if she was under the clutter. I checked her porch, but she didn't subscribe to the newspaper, and the Buddha wasn't talking.

My neighbor Sally was tending an outdoor shrine she kept in memory of one of her cats. There were some flowers, the cat's collar, a laminated photo of him, and a little terracotta urn. It was the saddest thing I'd ever seen. I started to weep.

Sally put a hand on my shoulder. "It's okay," she said. "He lived a long life. I'm trying to remember his good days."

"I think something's wrong with Venita."

"Yes," Sally agreed. "But I don't think there's anything we can do about that."

"No, I mean, something might have happened to her. She might end up like Richard."

"Why would you think that?"

I tried to come up with an answer that wouldn't sound incriminating. "I just haven't seen her around today," I said.

"That is rare," Sally said. "If there's anything Venita can be counted on for, it's to be around."

Back in our condo, Jamie brandished a handful of plastic bags and banana peels that raccoons had scattered onto our porch from Venita's debris piles. "This place," he said. "It was fine for a while, but now it's full of Venita. I'm going to talk to a realtor."

"We can't move now. I can barely move myself. We just need to adjust our expectations and live like Europeans do, all packed into tiny apartments, surrounded by eccentric neighbors." I'd been having intermittent contractions since dawn, and I didn't mention it because I'd felt contractions on and off for a week, and whenever I reported them, Jamie got too nervous to concentrate on his work. I'd tell him once they developed a rhythm. We needed to keep his job.

"You like it here," Jamie accused.

"Do not." I crossed my arms over my chest, resting them on the basketball. "You just want to take on a big mortgage so I can't stay home with the baby."

"Is that how you think of me?"

I looked off as another contraction came over me, feeling like the baby was balling up and taking my insides with her.

"I'm going to work," he said, grabbing his bag and jacket. "Avoid Venita."

A few hours later, warm fluid gushed between my legs. I consulted the thick, alarmist manual that the doctor had given me. The book said that once your water broke, the baby had to come out within twenty-four hours because of the risk of infection. I called my doctor, who told me to come to the hospital as soon as I could. Jamie didn't answer his phone at work and I could barely breathe enough to leave a message on his voice mail. I left a message on his boss's voice mail for good measure, but both of them were probably out for lunch. I changed clothes and wrapped a towel around my waist when I realized I'd wet myself again. I went outside on the porch, hoping I'd see Jamie approaching through the parking lot, which was empty except for my car, Venita's Impala, and four half-empty cans of paint that she was storing in front of it.

The contractions were only three minutes apart. How could I have thought the little pains I'd been feeling for weeks were anything like the real thing? I leaned against the spiky stucco wall outside as the next one came over me, closed my eyes and groaned, my toes curling.

"Are you all right?"

As the contraction subsided, I looked up to see Venita poking her head out of the Impala. So she'd survived her fall. There was a pile of trash next to the car: She'd been rummaging again. She looked like a sea hag I'd seen once in the fantasy-filled sketchbook of a guy who hung out at a bar I used to visit. Venita had a bandage on her forehead and her glasses were taped on one hinge. Something greasy was smeared on her sweatshirt and the sun caught its sheen.

My forehead was beaded with sweat and my legs shook. I planned to tell her that I was fine. Instead I said, "I think I need to go to the hospital."

"I can take you," she said, without hesitation.

I considered my options. I could wait for Jamie to check his messages and make the thirty-minute drive back from work, or I could call an ambulance. I had no idea if our insurance covered ambulance rides. Besides, summoning yet another ambulance to Casa del Rey felt like a bad beginning for our baby, and I couldn't wait any longer. My knees quaked from the pain. "Jamie didn't answer his phone," I explained. Venita nodded and patted my shoulder as if she'd heard this story before from other abandoned women in labor. She opened the Impala's passenger door, which looked like it might fall off its hinge. She stared into the car, fists on her hips, as she contemplated how to make room for me. Another contraction came and I squeezed my eyelids shut, shaking my head from side to side as I blew out a big breath of air. When I opened my eyes, there was a box from a ceiling fan, a spray bottle filled with green liquid, a turkey baster, a salad spinner, and a tangled pile of Ace bandages on the pavement next to the Impala. "Go ahead," she said, gesturing toward the passenger seat.

I put my towel on the ripped seat, in too much pain to feel ashamed, and eased myself down. I reached for the door handle.

"Careful," Venita said as she slid into the driver's seat.

I gently tugged the door closed. The Impala held together so precariously, its shell so thin, that I could distinguish individual pieces of gravel under the tires. From the rearview mirror dangled a scapular of Our Lady of Guadalupe and a pewter figure of Ganesh on a chain that swung with the motion of the car. A sticker of the Black Madonna was affixed to the bulging glove compartment, and three half-melted candles were melded to the dash. The drink holder contained a jar of flower potpourri and the sweet scent made me nauseous. I reached to roll down the window, but there was no handle. My next contraction hit as we rolled over the first speed bump.

"I'm going to puke," I said when I could speak.

Venita reached into the backseat and fished out a sticky Big Gulp cup, which she handed to me. I filled it. She made a right turn down the street. The hospital was less than a mile away. My muscles shook so fiercely that my teeth chattered and my mind drifted between contractions, flitting like a grasshopper. I moaned and thought of our college-girl neighbor. "How will I explain to the baby that some moans mean somebody is being beaten and you should call the cops, and others mean that the person is fine and wants to be left alone?" I asked Venita.

She glanced at me. "I've been in plenty of situations where I couldn't make that distinction myself."

"Have you ever had a baby?" I asked.

"Not that I know of," she said. "And I don't plan to. God knows how many times my mom told me she wished she'd never had me."

I looked at Venita, with her taped glasses, a scattered look in her eyes as she navigated the Impala over the road. Some mother's child, gone astray. I didn't want my baby to ever think of herself as a mistake. It hit me that if I didn't do right, I could wreck my baby's life, and for the first time I understood my parents' worry, their caution, the way they always did the safe, prudent, boring thing.

Another contraction began and I breathed through it. "It makes sense now," I said, "all the stuff in the Bible about childbirth being a punishment." I looked out the window. "I'm sorry."

"For what?" She flicked on the turn signal, which clicked a spastic double-time beat.

"It was me who kept calling the tow truck."

She laughed. "I was parking in your space. Who else would have done it?"

"Then why are you helping me?"

"Neighbors help."

"Why did you keep parking in my space when you knew I would tow your car?"

"I always meant to move it before you got home but then something would come up, and I'd need to haul something out of the house."

"You have too much stuff. It's holding you back."

"You sound like a mother."

We were headed east, stopped at a light a block before the railroad tracks. Just beyond them was the hospital. Once the baby was born, the years would begin to rush by at a heartbreaking clip, and the rush wouldn't end until she was grown and gone. Venita would stay Venita, reliably who she was, a steady if not stable presence against which to peg the blur of our child's life. A contraction started as Venita pressed the gas, the Impala bearing down on the railroad tracks, and I braced for the impact, for the new life that was coming, its end coiled somewhere tightly within its beginning.

Moonlight, Starlight, Boogie
Won't Be Out Tonight

They played the game in the darkened gym. The teacher chose the first boogie: Davonya Williams, slim and solemn and watchful, wearing pink teardrop eyeglasses, decades out of style. She lay on her stomach at the far end of the gym, head propped on cupped hands. She stared ahead as the other children drew near, skipping and chanting: "Moonlight, starlight, Boogie won't be out tonight," approaching her with each refrain. Chanting like that, skipping with such insouciance, they were asking for it, really, asking for anything that would come.

The rule was they had to skip forward until she rose, then run like hell to get away. If she touched them, they had to join her, become Boogie on the dark end of the gym. If they reached the wall that they started from, breathless, fingertips straining toward the cool, painted cinder blocks, they were safe. The lights flickered on, abolishing fear for the moment, but as they caught their breath, the children knew there would be more Boogies next time, and more the next.

The gym teacher always chose Davonya because she was the quickest, the most streamlined, hair corn-rowed tight to her head, each braid ending in three blue plastic beads held in place with a bit of tinfoil. The teacher knew she could rise from her stomach without an anticipatory twitch of a muscle and catch people as they fled, head start and all. She wore a discount store's knock-off version of Keds, held together by nothing but cheap glue, but they propelled her like the winged shoes of Mercury. The teacher dimmed the lights to give her a chance to surprise them with her opening sally, but she didn't need a chance, not really. She had speed, which was all the help she needed, and more than most were blessed with.

Davonya aimed for Katie Mills first, the second fastest girl. Katie was a pale, freckled child, with white blonde hair and the eyelashes of a fairy. Katie was always staring at Davonya with widened eyes, on edge, waiting for her to do something that would make her cry or scream, expecting it, though it never once happened. The only time Davonya ever touched her was during the game, and the Boogie-making gesture was more symbolic than harmful, just a sweep of thin fingers across Katie's back.

Katie's speed bothered Davonya most of all. Katie was skittish enough to sense a split second before everyone else when she should bolt. She had fretted all the meat off her bones and was down to muscle and spectral blond hair. Katie's mother dressed her in diaphanous pastel clothes that wouldn't weigh her down. Still, she was the best adversary available to Davonya. The other girls didn't care about running. They wore inappropriate shoes and let themselves be caught. The boys were faster, but still Davonya chased them down.

One day they played the game and Katie evaded Davonya's touch. She was so swift that she reached the wall every time, forcing Davonya to tag other children until her herd of Boogie underlings overwhelmed Katie, moving her to one side, slowing her advance so Davonya could catch her. Davonya didn't like to work that way, with so much help. It felt untidy.

For the first time that day Davonya felt the burden of the Boogie. When her dominance faltered, the fright she induced in the others went with it. The children joked with their friends, shoving each other into Davonya's path. Davonya didn't want to lose this, the only moments in her second-grade life when she felt powerful and intimidating, and so she ran faster.

The next time they played the game, when the gym teacher sized up the kids to select the Boogie, his glance fell not on Davonya, but on Katie, and he pointed. The children let out a collective gasp. Katie took the position, belly down against the cold floor on the dark side of the gym. Davonya stood in the middle of the pack on the opposite side, her arms across her chest. Pissed as she'd ever been. The other kids maintained a distance from her, as if her anger produced an electrical perimeter. When the children began to chant and skip toward Katie, taunting the Boogie, Katie rose and aimed for Davonya, chasing after her and tagging other children only incidentally, pursuing and unafraid.

Davonya felt a tinge of fear for once, the terror of the chased, but she wouldn't let herself be caught. She'd show the gym teacher his mistake. She and Katie played the game over and over, the other children all turned Boogie, running for a while with Katie and Davonya, then falling down one by one on the gritty lacquered floor in the dark of the gym, their breathing ragged as they waited for the game to end. But it went on, Katie pursuing, Davonya fleeing, always reaching the wall before Katie touched her.

The gym teacher ignored the complaints of the children and cracked open the door to the playground for some air, letting in the scent of fallen leaves rotting outside. He leaned against the wall, his whistle dangling from a chain around his neck, and watched the game continue. Davonya skipped aggressively; you couldn't really call it skipping, it bore such threat. He wanted to see how it would end.

The next time racing back across the gym floor, Davonya saw the open door and ran through it. Katie ran after her. The game had become too big for the gym. The gym teacher called for them to come back as they disappeared across the playground, puffs of schoolyard dust rising where their feet fell, but they didn't stop.

He jogged out after them and his knee buckled from an old high school football injury. He returned to the gym, pressed the office call button, and explained the situation before heading back outside to find the girls. The vice principal entered the gym where the kids coughed from their exertions, too dramatically, she thought. "That's enough," she said, turning on the lights.

The gym teacher walked around the perimeter of the school, looking for the girls. On a juniper bush by the flagpole, he noticed a bit of pink fluff, perhaps from Katie's sweater. In the gutter, he found a single blue plastic bead. He looked down the street across the way, saw a row of houses needing paint, slouching porches, untended yards. He took a tentative step across the deserted street. He never spent any time in this neighborhood outside of school hours, parking his car each morning in the locked lot. He thought of the meth house busts around here, the unprovoked shootings, the strange case of a man two blocks away who'd taken in a boarder, then dismembered him and set the house on fire to hide what he'd done. It was time to call the parents, then the cops.

But when he went to the office to make the calls, the principal told him that the girls had turned up in their next class, scratches on their faces, bits of dead leaves in their hair, Katie's sweater stretched out, Davonya's shirt ripped, their nostrils flaring as they took their seats, still out of breath. They wouldn't discuss what happened, wouldn't tell anyone where they went. *Who won?* was all the kids wanted to know. But neither girl would speak.

In college, Davonya eases into the starting blocks. Her muscles twitch once before they must be silent and wait to explode. Davonya wears contact lenses—the donated Lions Club eyeglasses far behind her—and shoes bearing symbols that denote speed, a swoosh or three slashes ranked on either side like the gills of a shark. She can hear the others breathing, adjusting their positions on either side of her. But her eyes face straight ahead. Her chin hovers near her left knee as she waits, crouched, for the starter to call *Set*. Sometimes her thoughts wander to the game she played as a girl, the game that set her on this course. What was the gym teacher thinking when he came up with it? Had he forgotten how scary it was to chant an invitation to a monster, how children magnified every threat in the funhouse mirror of their minds? Or did he feel assured that these were city kids, clad in a tough rind of half-neglect, and their parents would never ask what games they'd played in gym that day, let alone be moved to complain? Maybe he chose that game of tag because the person designated *It* became a luminary instead of a pariah.

The starter calls set and Davonya rises, arching her back, suspending her body in the awkward pose that says: *Let me run.* The gun, and she bursts forward, trying not to uncoil too soon but to use it, to exploit the momentum as she draws herself to full height, arms pumping. The lone trace of discernible fat on her body—in her cheeks—quivers as her feet pound. Her track spikes dig into the spongy, brick-colored surface, giving her a little push with each step. She is in a center lane and sees no one in front of her, and that is the way she likes it. The gym teacher, so long ago, taught her at least one thing: that there were still times, in the modern world, when self-preservation depended on how quickly you could run.

La Sexycana

When Charlotte searched the internet for Araceli Ramirez, the girl she'd mentored for six years, she discovered "La Sexycana." In her profile photo, Araceli wore a baseball cap knocked to the side, her plump, glossy lips puckered, prepared to spit or bestow a kiss.

"So that's what happened to your girl," Charlotte's friend Leo Cruz said, looking over her shoulder. Charlotte needed to write a concert preview for *Denver Details*, the alternative weekly newspaper they worked for, but the boss was out so they were goofing off in Charlotte's office.

Charlotte studied photos of Araceli in hot pants, displaying her cleavage, and one of her with a blank-faced lug, apparently naked in bed, which were interspersed with images of women in lingerie, riding men stripped to their waists, their abs rippling. Charlotte sipped her tea and scrolled through the strange declarations that festooned La Sexycana's page in noisy fonts: "Good Girls Gotta Get Down Wit Da Gangstas," "I Kiss Girls," and "Ain't no one on the corner got swagger like my blood." Music thumped and signs flashed—it was like a dance club in there.

Charlotte shook her head. "Last thing I knew she was this smart young lady with a full ride to college, and now she's a sex worker."

"No, that's just the way kids present themselves these days." Leo would know—he handled sales for the sex ads in the back of *Denver Details*.

"When I was her age, smart women didn't want to be seen that way," Charlotte said, thinking of the unsexy flannel she'd layered herself with in college. "And I'm only ten years older than Araceli!"

"Generation gaps spring up quicker now."

"Someday twins born minutes apart won't have anything to say to each other."

"See, look here," Leo said, "under the row of fluorescent booze bottles, it says, 'this bitch has the intelligence to complement the beauty, and I'm a junior at Metro State, so watch out stoopid tricks!'"

"Why must she call herself 'bitch'?" But at least Araceli was still in college. "At the top it says, 'Ima be up at LimeLite on Friday, partying. Don't U wish U were me?' That's dangerous. Anyone could see this." It felt wrong to let Leo look at pictures of Araceli dressed like that. "I could go to LimeLite and warn her not to post where she's going to be."

Leo glanced at Charlotte with the amused look he often gave her. "LimeLite is not for you. No one there hangs out drinking Jack and listening to tortured rockers."

Charlotte scrutinized the dense, uncapitalized, casually spelled block of text on the right side of La Sexycana's page. It contained all the answers to the questions she'd been asking since Araceli stopped responding to her phone calls and emails, written with the unflagging confidence of someone who'd yet to work a full-time job. A lot of La Sexycana's diatribe was addressed to an unnamed "you" that might well have been Charlotte. "I'm a celebrity in my life, while you just live in yourz." Well, that was accurate. "I have big plans, goals, and places to go. You might be working for me some day, so play nice bichez!" So she was still ambitious. "I may be the most intelligent and beautiful woman you've come across, but I can get down!" Charlotte glanced at the *Consumer Reports* next to her on the table, open to the back page with its humorous packaging misprints that she'd been chuckling over before she'd discovered La Sexycana. Charlotte no longer got down.

Charlotte earned a journalism degree in college and then returned home to Denver, where she found a job editing the events calendar for *Denver Details*, a meaningless position she mistakenly assumed she'd soon rise above. She organized and typed in information from clubs, bars, and concert venues about events around town. She also performed miscellaneous tasks for the other staff members: archiving past issues, dealing with advertiser requests, fetching aspirin for the rock critic.

Seven employees worked at the office, which claimed the first two floors of a lavender Victorian house near downtown Denver. The boss, a gum-snapping, fast-talker named Barry, was too cheap to hire a cleaning service, so the toilets were never scrubbed and the bathroom trash overflowed until someone got drunk and emptied it. The boss instructed Charlotte to dress "grungy," and she was covered in newsprint smudges from the tear sheets she sent out to advertisers.

On the third day of work, Charlotte watched as Barry handed Leo a fluorescent flier. "This is from Suzy's House of Pleasure, a new joint on Colfax. Hit them up for an ad, Cruz."

"You're always one step ahead," Leo said, taking the flier. "That's why our paper catches the pulse of the city."

Barry patted Leo on the back like a favorite son, and then went to lunch.

Leo caught Charlotte staring. "I know what you're thinking," he whispered as he approached her desk. "I'm a kiss-ass. But you'd better start doing the same if you want to get into sales."

"Sales?" Charlotte said, gathering her long hair with a rubber band so it wouldn't get caught when she had to heave a box. "I'd rather write or edit."

Leo shook his head. "Then I'll buy you lunch. You're going to be broke forever."

Leo never had to actually buy anything. His wallet brimmed with comp passes and gift certificates from various ad deals he'd worked with restaurants and clubs, and who knew what else, given the content of the back-page ads. He was toothpaste-commercial handsome, so that Charlotte barely registered him when they met, recording him as a blur of dark hair, white teeth, and brown skin. His dress shirts, hair, and pants had a sheen to them and he didn't seem to sweat, even as they toiled in July without air conditioning.

They ate at a sushi place near the office and Leo told her stories about Barry. "His house is sick," Leo explained. "But he's got leopard print everything. It draws in putas galore. And not young ones." Leo asked if Charlotte had a boyfriend and she said they'd just broken up. When she asked Leo if he had a girlfriend, he said, "At the moment? Three."

Until Leo asked her to lunch, Charlotte didn't realize how lonely she'd been during the few months since she'd graduated from college. The friends she'd grown up with had moved away.

Back at the office, Charlotte set to work tearing out pages from the latest issue to mail to clients. Then she saw it: a public service ad that sought mentors for the Bridges to Tomorrow Foundation. A middle-aged white professional man beamed next to a clean-cut Latino boy, who looked up at him with admiration. She should do something useful with her time until she moved up the hierarchy at work. She liked kids—she could hang out with one, help her with her studies, send her on her way. Anyone could do Charlotte's job, but not just anyone would mentor a kid. Charlotte could do at least one good thing until the day she'd be writing for *Rolling Stone*.

"I don't pay you to *read* the paper," Barry yelled as he barreled by.

Charlotte set the mentoring ad aside. But that night when she sat at home in her quiet apartment while her neighbors partied in the courtyard outside, she dialed the number of the foundation.

After Charlotte completed the background check and interview, she met with the director of the mentoring organization, Peter, an earnest, pink-skinned young man in round glasses. "We accept kids into the program in sixth grade," he explained, "and if they complete all the requirements through middle school, the foundation pays for prep school." They selected the brightest poor kids in the city through a rigorous interview process. He showed Charlotte profiles of some children, with their ages, hobbies, academic record, and a photocopied picture. All the kids liked hanging out at the mall and rooting for the Denver Nuggets. She'd have to judge them by their photos. There was a chubby girl with a sweet smile named Rosa who seemed like she'd be easy to win over. Araceli had sharp features, and her dead-on gaze at the camera looked determined. She was going places, like Charlotte wished she were. Charlotte hesitated over Rosa, then picked Araceli.

At the Bridges end-of-summer picnic, Charlotte wore a Sleater-Kinney T-shirt and wondered if she'd have instilled more confidence if she'd worn a suit, as other mentors had, straight from work. But she didn't own a suit. She sat next to the Ramirez family, trying to eat chicken wings coated in over-sweetened barbecue sauce without smearing it all over her face, making nervous small talk about whatever came into her head.

"It's too bad the Nuggets didn't make it to the playoffs," Charlotte ventured.

"They usually don't," Araceli said.

"Celi!" her mom, Jolene, said. "Use your manners." Jolene's tight

T-shirt indented where her bra cut into her soft flesh. She had puffy eyelids and a down-turned mouth. "We're so thankful Araceli got into this program," she said, resting a hand on Charlotte's forearm.

"She must be a very smart girl," Charlotte said.

Araceli was tiny, with delicate wrists, slender, long-fingered hands, and dark, glossy hair that hung all the way down her back. Some of the other girls had begun the grim descent into puberty, but Araceli still looked like a kid, which comforted Charlotte. A kid would be easier to bond with than a teenager. Araceli and her friends wore T-shirts studded with rhinestones that declared their preciousness, spelling out "Princess" and "Angel" and "Sweetie Pie."

"Are you going anywhere before school starts?" Charlotte asked, then rebuked herself. Maybe poor people couldn't go on vacation.

"Probably to Albuquerque to see our family," Araceli said, taking a small bite of her sloppy barbecue and then pressing her paper napkin to her mouth.

"Last year we went to Hawaii," Jolene said.

"I've never been to Hawaii," Charlotte said, with too much surprise.

Before the afternoon was over, Jolene told Charlotte how she'd never married Araceli's father, who turned up every once in a while, how they'd cut back her hours as a receptionist at an appliance repair shop—"For $8 an hour I have to listen to people yell at me about their dishwashers"—how they owned a flock of birds and went to monthly bird club meetings at which everyone entered a raffle for a parrot. Araceli kept her eyes down as her mother spilled all this. Even at twelve, Araceli was circumspect, never filling an awkward silence. She wasn't like Rosa, who sat at the next table over, desperately shy but wanting to please.

Charlotte had trouble arranging the first outing, as Araceli's family didn't own an answering machine, and when someone did pick up the phone, it was a deep-voiced man who said, *"Bueno?"* over the sound of riotous birdcalls.

After three weeks, the director helped arrange a meeting. "Araceli's family needs to make this happen," Paul told Charlotte. "Meeting regularly with a mentor is part of our scholarship agreement."

As Charlotte drove Araceli to the zoo, she checked her blind spot three times before changing lanes and drove five miles under the speed limit. She had never driven a kid in her car before. Charlotte didn't know what to say, so she kept talking and talking. "Sometimes I get concert tickets from work," she said. "Would you like to go see Destiny's Child?" She had no idea if she could make this happen. One time Leo had passed her some tickets to The Shins at the Gothic Theatre. Charlotte wasn't supposed to take her mentee to expensive activities. "No cash gifts," the handbook also said. But Charlotte would have slipped the girl a twenty if it would expedite the bonding process.

"I love Beyoncé," Araceli said with enthusiasm, turning to look up at Charlotte.

"Me too," Charlotte said. She had put the radio on the hip-hop station before she picked Araceli up, and felt like a fool. At a meeting, one of the other mentors had complained her mentee always turned the channel to rap, riddled with misogynist lyrics. Charlotte just wished someday Araceli would be comfortable enough to reach out and change the station.

It was early August and the temperature hit a hundred. The animals hid themselves or lay belly up in the dirt of their enclosures, a tail twitching now and then. The tiger paced back and forth in his outdoor cage, boredom on four paws. Depressed, slumping mothers pushed their toddlers around in strollers with elaborate canopies, and no one seemed to be having any fun except the teenagers who worked at the snack booths, who laughed and cast electric glances at each other, sly and sexy, animated alone among all the basking beasts and sauntering people. Araceli watched the teenagers and stayed silent, so Charlotte kept up an inane patter. "The monkeys are my favorite. Especially the Golden Lion Tamarins."

Charlotte led Araceli to the cafeteria and told her to order whatever she wanted, gesturing expansively at the burgers and hot dogs that had been sitting in their foil wrappers for hours. Charlotte paid for their meals and Araceli didn't say thank you. That was the first time mentoring made Charlotte feel both magnanimous and cranky, and that she detected a reciprocal feeling of mild hatred toward her in Araceli.

Eventually, after some walks, a drive to see aspen leaves in the foothills, and a few meals together, Araceli began to talk to Charlotte. She wanted to be a veterinarian. She owned five Chow dogs and dozens of birds. She didn't like math. But she never asked Charlotte about herself. True, she was just a kid, but Charlotte expected Araceli would have questions. What was college like? What did she do at work? Charlotte occasionally delivered little speeches she hoped were informative. "Sometimes you have to take an entry level position in a field you're interested in and work your way up," Charlotte said, hoping this sounded sage and true.

Charlotte was worried she wasn't doing the right thing. She told Leo she'd buy him a six pack if he came with her to a mentor meeting, posing as a potential volunteer, though given his occupation he'd never make it past the screening process.

"Look at these mentors," Charlotte whispered. Most were middle-aged professionals who worked for Lambert Funds, a local investment bank whose owner was a program sponsor. "They reek success."

"My kind of folks," Leo said, "out to help *mi gente*." He nodded and grinned at anyone who met his glance. The other mentors were eager to see Leo, as most of them were white.

The program director approached Charlotte. "It'd be great to have some of the kids who are aspiring journalists visit you at work someday."

"Sure," Charlotte said, hoping he hadn't heard Leo's stifled laugh. Their office wasn't sanitary enough for a child to visit.

When the director walked away, Leo whispered, "Where did he get the idea that you're a journalist?"

"Same place my mom got it, I guess." Her title was the "Calendar Editor." She wasn't a reporter, so what was she? A typist, really. That was kind of quaint at least. "Maybe I should quit, so Araceli could hook up with a lawyer."

"Oh no. You can't quit on the kid now until she's thirty," Leo said. "Her dad's already ditched her, right? You need to stick around and be there when she baptizes her triplets."

"So I'd be like a spinster aunt?"

"You'd be the best spinster aunt. All you have to be is one rung above the other adults in this kid's life. You have a college degree."

"Yay me." Still, it would be kind of noble if Charlotte simply remained in Araceli's life, a stalwart presence at games and graduations, there to listen to Araceli's dreams and fears.

Peter invited mentors to ask questions or mention techniques that had worked for them. Charlotte held up her hand. "Araceli doesn't talk to me much," she said.

"That's a common problem at the beginning," Peter said, nodding. "Does anyone have suggestions?" A brassy woman in the front row took the mic and launched into a monologue. She often fetched her mentee from school, and together they cooked dinner, watched movies, braided each other's hair, and engaged in meaningful discussions. The girl had raised her grades from C's to A's. "It's really not as hard as it seems at first," the woman concluded. Leo elbowed Charlotte and whispered, "You're *failing* the future of America."

This was how it was supposed to work—a kid who was edging down the wrong path nudged back in line by the care and love of a responsible adult. Which Charlotte supposedly was.

Araceli's math grades slipped her last semester of eighth grade, and Charlotte began to help with homework once a week, visiting Araceli's house, sandwiched between two highways, where she lived with three adults, including an ancient uncle who never left his bedroom while Charlotte was there. Jolene collected big-eyed dolls from flea markets, and they stood ranked about the house, mounted on stands in their elaborate Scarlet O'Hara or Pocahontas get-ups. Charlotte and Araceli worked at a crowded table near the kitchen, the television blaring nearby. An oversized cage with two-dozen finches chattered by the front door. They were just studying fractions at Araceli's poor Catholic school, but she'd have to dive into Algebra the next year at the expensive all-girls prep school the foundation was paying for her to attend. Helping Araceli with her math often felt like the only thing of value Charlotte did all day. "See," Charlotte said as Araceli reworked a problem, "isn't it nice how there's always one right answer? You just have to find it."

Charlotte hoped perfect math papers were a way to fight against the chaos of Araceli's life. Araceli's Nino had cancer, her mother's asthma troubled her, some dogs rampaged into their garage and killed their lovebirds, homework was lost, actually eaten by a dog or thrown away by her uncle, they didn't have the money to buy

Araceli the calculator she would need for Algebra and didn't have any number 2 pencils to use on a test. *Where did you even buy number 1 or 3 pencils?* Charlotte thought. She brought over two packs of pencils from the supply closet at work.

Araceli wanted to do well—that's why the foundation had selected her. She bought a sweatshirt embroidered with the name of her future high school, St. Anne's, and wore it on chilly days. As they worked together, Araceli made progress, and she brought her corrected tests and papers to show Charlotte. "The teacher said my boa constrictor essay was the best one in class," Araceli said, holding the paper up. "You see," Charlotte said, "you can do this." Araceli smiled as Charlotte crowed over her work, Charlotte thinking that's all they had to do, turn those Cs into As and a golden road to college and beyond would follow.

The summer after Araceli finished eighth grade, Leo gave Charlotte two passes to the Destiny's Child concert in Magness Arena.

Araceli wore lipstick and an ice-blue shirt with a glittery shooting star over her still-girlish chest. She chattered about her pets as they drove across town and complained of boredom, having nothing to do but watch TV and feed the animals. "The summer is too long," Araceli said. "I can't wait to start high school."

"You're ready," Charlotte said, worried Araceli's sad middle school hadn't prepared her for St. Anne's. "You'll do great."

The arena was filled with young girls and their parents, each girl in the tightest shirt her mom would allow, designer jeans and leopard-print jackets, skirts with fringe, glitter, and tufts of fake pink fur. The parents chatted with each other while the girls riveted their attention to the stage, even though the house lights were still on. Now and then a spontaneous squeal unleashed. White girls with money, Charlotte thought, the kind Araceli would have to deal with in a few months.

Charlotte and Araceli stood in the press box above the stage with a handful of middle-aged reporters, who sat, grim-faced, taking notes on the proceedings below like they were watching a political coup. The lights dimmed and Destiny's Child came out in a burst of sequins, the three women each in a unique dress made out of the same shiny, aqua snake-print fabric. They took turns singing the lead under the spotlight, dancing in six-inch heels, but Beyoncé was the star, strong and goddess tall, her hair flying, her voice soaring, a woman teaching an audience of girls what they wanted to be.

Charlotte somehow knew most of Destiny's Child's songs and she learned all Beyoncé had to do to make the arena erupt was raise one eyebrow. Charlotte and Araceli were the only people dancing in the press box. By the end all the reporters shuffled off to file their stories before deadline, and it was just Charlotte and Araceli, hoarse with screaming through the encores. When Charlotte walked Araceli to her door, Araceli surprised Charlotte with a quick hug before going inside. She smelled like baby powder and night air. "Thanks," Araceli said, "my friends will be so jealous." Charlotte stood on the porch for a moment after the door closed, her cheeks warm, a happy buzz inside her chest.

At St. Anne's, Araceli became the dumb kid. In her old school she had earned As without having learned to punctuate a sentence or master multiplication and division. A few months into high school, she had a D in Spanish. Although she could speak fluently, she couldn't write or conjugate a verb. The words she knew were not on the tests. Her family said *carro* instead of *coche*. When one quiz asked her where to purchase a stamp, she had no idea, and guessed the bank. And Araceli didn't understand that answering a question correctly was different than answering what the teacher wanted. There were only a handful of other Latinas at the school, all of them sponsored by the foundation, and Charlotte tried but couldn't really understand what this meant to Araceli. Charlotte offered to help her more often with homework, but with Araceli's twice daily forty-minute commute between the extreme north and south sides of Denver, she was exhausted.

During the spring of Araceli's ninth-grade year, Jolene opened the door for Charlotte. "I am so mad," Jolene said. "There's a girl teasing Celi at school—saying 'I can't believe she's in high school if she's so flat.'" Jolene dropped her voice to a whisper. "Now they're calling her Tortilla."

"That's terrible," Charlotte said, thinking about how she as the mentor should respond. Should she tell Araceli that the breasts would come, and that meanwhile she should be out there enjoying the lack of their burden, running wind sprints every day?

"It's a girl's school," Jolene continued. "You'd think no one would talk about boobs. But they get these ideas from watching the T.V., all those commercials with subliminal messages."

"Girls can be vicious," Charlotte said. "I'll talk to her."

"Would you? It's so great she has you. I never did Algebra or went to private school."

The faith Jolene placed in Charlotte made her uncomfortable.

Araceli came out of her room with red, puffy eyes. Charlotte hugged her, and Araceli felt small and thin, angles and bones. She accepted the embrace but pulled away quickly.

They drove down the street to the library to work on Araceli's homework. It was a beautiful March day. Some kids from North High were hanging out in front of the library, the girls not wearing enough clothes, their arms goosefleshed, the boys hidden in their hoodies. There wasn't a book or backpack between them.

"It's hard to study when it's nice outside," Araceli said, watching the public school kids flirt. "And I never get it right anyway."

"Sure you do," Charlotte said. "You're getting better in math every day. And your writing is so good." At least it was after Charlotte corrected the text-message speak in it. Araceli's papers on *The Grapes of Wrath* and *The House on Mango Street* were sensitive and thoughtful, more insightful, Charlotte felt certain, than those of her classmates who'd never experienced lack or pain. As they walked inside the library, Charlotte shifted their talk to Araceli's future. "Are you still thinking of going out of state for college?" Once Araceli had mentioned that she'd like to go to Texas Christian University, like one of the older girls from the foundation.

"Last year I knew where I wanted to go and what I wanted to be," Araceli said as she dropped into a library chair. "But now I don't know any of that."

Charlotte hated to see this go-get-'em girl so dispirited at fifteen. She wondered if Araceli would have been better off at a school in her own neighborhood. The scholarship gave her a chance to make it out, but who wanted to make it out if it only meant a lifetime spent dealing with horrible white girls?

The next week when Charlotte came to pick up Araceli for tutoring, she wasn't home. Charlotte sat on the couch, chatting with Jolene until Araceli came in the door, crying. She wore a red shirt decorated with rhinestones in an emanating heart pattern, and her long hair trailed behind her as she flew around, blowing her nose and collecting her schoolbooks.

"What's wrong, hija?" Jolene said.

"These girls say I cheated." Araceli had to give a presentation in Social Studies. She and Chelsea, another girl working on the same topic, met with the teacher together to discuss ideas for their presentations, and they had both done what the teacher advised and used the same sources. Chelsea gave her presentation first. "And when I went, the CD player didn't work," Araceli said.

"Would it help if I went out and bought you a CD player?" Jolene asked.

"It's too late," Araceli snapped. "These girls started talking about how I ripped off Chelsea's report."

"Chelsea complained?" Charlotte asked.

"No, she's nice. It's these other girls who all went to middle school together. This one girl, Katelyn, told the teacher that she saw me taking notes during Chelsea's presentation."

"Katelyn!" Jolene said. "She's the same one that calls you—"

"Right," Araceli said, cutting her off.

"But you read it out for me, Celi," Jolene said. "You did your own work."

"Let's go to the library," Araceli said to Charlotte. She wore a hard expression, like she was pissed and embarrassed that Charlotte had seen her emotions.

"Let me guess," Charlotte said as they drove to the library. "The girl you're accused of cheating off—the nice one—is popular."

Araceli nodded.

"And the one who accused you—Katelyn—she's farther down in her group, like number three or four?"

"Yes," she said.

"And a little fat?" Charlotte imagined an insecure girl with ample breasts, out to demolish the weak, a tattletale, pointing out who was flat, who had cheated.

"A little."

"She's just making a power play. Trying to move up rank by doing something to impress the popular girl. Why don't I talk to your teacher? Or the director of Bridges—he can discuss it with the principal."

"No," Araceli said. "I can handle it myself."

But Charlotte did mention it to Peter. Araceli had worked hard to get where she was and Charlotte wasn't going to let some privileged twit interfere with her progress. She told Peter not to say anything, but the principal summoned Araceli for a meeting and allowed her to write a paper to make up for the presentation grade.

The next time Charlotte picked up Araceli, she barely spoke. Charlotte kept glancing over at her, asking about the make-up paper, but Araceli kept her eyes focused out her window.

"What do you have today?" Charlotte asked at the library, expecting the usual load of papers, math, and science reports.

"Ten math problems," Araceli said, dropping her Algebra book on the table.

"That's all?" Charlotte asked.

Araceli took out a piece of paper and whipped through the problems, then shoved them toward Charlotte, who checked her work before driving Araceli home. That had been the turning point, Charlotte saw now. They'd begun revealing themselves to each other and then Araceli shut herself off.

Araceli made excuses to avoid meeting with Charlotte for tutoring and she worked like a soldier to prove to Peter that she didn't need help. She raised her grades to As and Bs. She went to dances at a public school near where she lived, hung out with kids from her own neighborhood, made it so that Charlotte was the only white person she had to see outside of school hours. She started talking about majoring in Chicano studies in college, so Charlotte took her to see a play at El Centro Su Teatro, Denver's long-running Chicano theater. At one point Charlotte mentioned that she'd studied in England for a semester in college, and suggested Araceli try something like that. "I'm not interested in Europe," she said flatly.

Junior year Araceli's breasts came in and her hips flared out. Her legs were long, her hair like a little girl's fantasy of a mermaid's tresses. She passed the bulky St. Anne's sweatshirt to Jolene. At school there was a dress code, but after hours Araceli wore clothes that plunged and clung, carried a purse in the shape of a black lace bustier.

The foundation required them to meet twice a month but eased this rule when the kids became busy with high school activities. By senior year, Araceli kept telling Charlotte she was too busy to meet, with SAT prep and required volunteer work to complete. Charlotte had spent so much time helping Araceli over the past five years that she didn't know how to fill the missing chunks in her week. Charlotte had boyfriends now and then, who'd stick around only long enough to prevent Charlotte from working up the nerve to move to New York and land a real writing job. Occasionally, Araceli would email her a draft of an essay she wanted help with, and Charlotte would type up her comments. "Well thanx for looking over it. Talk to you later. Bye," she wrote back. When colleges accepted Araceli, she sent word in a group email to Charlotte, Peter, and a few other people in the foundation. Reading the email, Charlotte felt proud, then stung. Why couldn't Araceli have called with the news?

"Can I take you out to celebrate?" Charlotte emailed back. "Beyoncé is playing the Pepsi Center." Charlotte scored tickets more easily now because she had begun to fill in for the paper's concert reviewer on shows he didn't care to see.

As they waited for the concert to begin, Charlotte peppered Araceli with questions about college and the full-ride scholarships she'd been offered. Araceli dispatched the questions, and then the lights went down. Beyoncé had gone solo and everyone else on stage danced in her service, providing a distraction while she changed outfits. Beyoncé would reappear, wearing a golden, sequin-spangled bodysuit, or a white, flowing jacket with shoulder pads and a billowing cape, or a silver mini-dress that looked like it was covered with diamonds. Araceli clapped for each song, but didn't cheer or dance as she had before. So Charlotte refrained from dancing, remembering that she didn't like this kind of music anyway. After that, Charlotte attended Araceli's graduation, and the last sign she had of Araceli was when she cashed the $100 check for her graduation, money Charlotte could have spent on a new set of tires for her old car.

After Charlotte discovered La Sexycana's page, she checked it every night before going to bed, trying to decode it. "I Be Gettin Haterz Like You Wudnt Believe, So Wassup? Ima Walk It Like I Talk It So You Bitchez Dont Forget It." What if some perverted freak or one of those haterz read Araceli's LimeLite post and tried to find her? Charlotte sat up in her chair and pulled her robe tighter. She called Leo.

"You need to let that girl go," he said over the crowd noise in a bar.

"Anybody could be reading her website."

"Like you?"

"Like someone who means her harm. I'm going to LimeLite."

Leo paused, then said, "You don't have the clothes."

"I'm not going to dance."

"No, I mean, you have to look a certain way to get past the bouncer."

Leo made her bring the clothes she'd wear into work so he could approve them. She pulled out a pair of fishnet pantyhose from her backpack, and Leo laughed. "That's something a Disneyland hooker would wear. Do you have a cancan dress in there?"

"Fine. You tell me what to wear."

"Get some kind of tight black stuff. I know these people, I'll get you in."

"You could have offered that before you made me bring these clothes to work."

"But we had fun."

Downtown on Friday night, glinting black SUVs and Hondas with gleaming rims and spoilers cruised Market Street, and people lined up outside the clubs, the crowd from the rooftop patios filling the night with chatter.

"Sexycana needs some better taste," Leo said. "It's all putas and frat boys out here. Or whatever you call frat boys who haven't been to college."

The women lined up at LimeLite dressed like La Sexycana. Charlotte wore a black dress several inches shorter than felt comfortable and she was so aware of the way the neckline slightly exposed her cleavage that she kept ducking her chin to look at it. Maybe that's what it felt like to be a guy. She'd followed makeup tips from a magazine of the sort she usually disdained to read, but still, she didn't belong here. She'd thought mentoring was a fool-proof do-good thing, that the kid was bound to need you. But maybe Araceli never had.

"Hey baby," Leo said, circumventing the line and slapping the beefy bouncer's hand. "Can we get in?"

"Sure thang." The bouncer unhooked a chain. He had a shaved head and rolls of neck fat. "Reginald," he said, extending his hand to Charlotte.

"Char—" Charlotte said, shaking his hand, still dazzled by Leo's ability to cut the line, "Charo."

Reginald drew her hand to his mouth and kissed it.

"What was that?" Charlotte whispered as she and Leo entered the club.

"You look good, girl. Shit, I'd sleep with Charo."

"Get in line."

"That's La Sexycana talking."

The club was half empty, the music reverberating in the dark, warehouse-like space. Charlotte headed straight for the bar.

"I thought you were going to be the super mentor," Leo said as she ordered a frozen strawberry margarita.

"I need to get my courage up."

"Twelve," the bartender said.

"Twelve *dollars*?" Charlotte asked.

"I got it." Leo threw a comp drink voucher down on the bar. He poked her shoulder, whispering, "Tip the dude. I can't bring you anywhere."

She sat down and sucked the drink through her straw. "Where is she?"

"Up dancing in one of those cages, if she walks like she talks."

"No mentee of mine is dancing in a damn cage."

"The foundation should have a new motto: keeping girls off the pole since 1999."

Three women in tight skirts and torturous heels with lioness hair minced up to the bar, and Leo tossed Charlotte a few drink tickets before approaching them. She didn't want Leo to leave her alone, but what could she expect? He was Leo. At least he'd come with her.

After three free margaritas, Charlotte's mouth puckered from the sweetness and a headache pulsed in the center of her forehead, keeping time with the music. Leo cavorted with the women on the dance floor that was beginning to fill. Charlotte imagined what it would feel like to dance like that, with such abandon, free of her mind for once. Beyoncé's voice rang out over a bumptious bass line, and Charlotte felt a rush of nostalgia for the twelve-year-old Araceli had been. Quiet, innocent, doll-loving, protector of birds and dogs, full of dreams, almost prim. Then Araceli had run into Charlotte and decided to go the other way.

Charlotte was just about to start sucking down the next margarita when she saw her. Not Araceli, but La Sexycana. She flowed up to the bar in a clinging mini-dress that looked made of silver tinsel. She was four inches taller, owing to her gleaming heels. Her hair trailed behind her the way supermodels' did in photo shoots with blowing fans. Her face was a perfect mask, fierce and marvelous. It wasn't just a boast: she really was a celebrity in her life. Charlotte slid off her stool and pushed through the crowd of young men and women that surrounded La Sexycana. Charlotte couldn't stop herself from reaching out to touch Araceli's chiseled cheek. Araceli knocked her hand away.

"Can I help you?" Her mouth reared into the kiss/spit look she wore in her profile photo.

"Celi," Charlotte said, thinking about how so many hours over six years could mean so much to her and nothing to Araceli.

She studied Charlotte's face for a moment. "You go to clubs?"

"I knew you'd be here because you wrote about it online."

"You read my page."

"It's public."

"So you're stalking me?"

"You shouldn't tell people where you're going to be, especially since your page is so—" she sought the right word, "provocative."

Araceli's hand flew up to dismiss her. "Still trying to lecture me. I only met with you because I had to for the scholarship." She turned toward the bar and commanded a guy with a slim fox face to get out some cash.

Charlotte was half numbed by alcohol but still felt this blow. "You wouldn't have gotten the scholarship if I hadn't helped you pass through ninth grade," Charlotte said.

"Anybody could have done that."

"But not just anybody did," Charlotte said, "I did." Charlotte felt one more mentor speech welling up inside her. She wanted to tell Araceli that after you were out of school, it wasn't as easy to achieve what you wanted. You were no longer anybody's star. You started grungy, in some back room, doing the tasks that no one else wanted to do, and maybe if you did that right, someone would give you a better chance. Or maybe not.

"Is she bothering you?" La Sexycana's fox-faced attendant asked her.

"I can handle her," Araceli said.

"You can *handle* me?"

"Hey, look," Araceli said, softening, like she knew that if she pissed Charlotte off she could tell everyone about the dolls and birds and dogs and veterinarian dreams. "I don't want to fight with you. I appreciate what you did. But we don't need each other anymore."

Charlotte nodded. "Fair enough." Maybe Araceli was right that Charlotte had needed her more. By now Charlotte knew she'd never write for *Rolling Stone*. She'd used mentoring Araceli through high school as an excuse to stay in Denver but the truth was that she'd been too afraid to leave her hometown. Now she'd be at *Denver Details* until it folded, which looked imminent, Barry continually reducing its paper and print size to cut costs until it vaporized out of existence.

"Well, good to see you," Araceli said with a flat voice that indicated the opposite before her friends led her back onto the dance floor.

What had Charlotte been hoping for? Did she want Araceli to dress conservatively, stop flaunting her looks, get some sort of office job and settle into the long grind of adulthood without ever screwing up? Rosa graduated the same year as Araceli, a bookish girl, the daughter of Mexican immigrants who didn't speak English, and Peter told her she'd landed a full ride to the University of Denver. She displayed the tense line-toeing of second-generation kids, majoring in engineering: she couldn't afford to fail. But Araceli had the cushion of her beauty, the same confidence of those white girls that bedeviled her in high school.

"Was that your girl?" Leo asked, squeezing Charlotte's shoulder. He was out of breath and for the first time since Charlotte had known him, a little sweaty. "I was about to get her number."

"Don't bother. She wouldn't call you back."

"Do you want to leave?" He looked concerned.

That wasn't like Leo, especially not on a Friday night. Maybe La Sexycana was right. Here Charlotte was out at a club, all dressed up, and she was the only person not having fun. "Charo is going to stay," Charlotte said, wiping some margarita remnants off her mouth with a napkin. The alcohol made her stop worrying about her short skirt and cleavage. She took Leo's hand. "Are you going to dance with me, or do I have to go find Reginald?"

Leo led the way. Charlotte copied Leo's moves, invented some of her own, and danced until her hair stuck to her face with sweat. As the night wore on, they moved closer to each other, and when

Leo kissed her, Charlotte grabbed his ass. As they danced, Charlotte didn't worry about consequences or setting an example. Araceli would figure things out. Just as Charlotte figured out that doing something the whole world claimed to believe was worthwhile didn't actually mean that it was.

Last Summer's Song

You are last summer's song, and on this summer's airwaves, you are a cheap trick, an invitation to premature nostalgia. You are an aftertaste, not an heirloom: recognize the fact. You are last summer's song, your welcome is outworn, your moment has passed, your fifteen minutes are up. Last summer you made sandy toes tap and carpool mothers sing. You induced us to take each other's hands, or to raise our own, to stretch them, fingers wide, toward the sun. You made friends exchange conspirators' smiles and reach, in tandem, to turn the radio up.

We, the people of skin the collective shade of mid-summer brown, looked better than we usually did, listening to you. We looked like people one could, theoretically, love.

You made us feel summer to the marrow, quickened hearts under edgeless swaths of blue sky, made us forget carcinogenic implications, bask in the heat and worship the sun. You blared out of ballpark speakers as baseball's archetypal crowd montage cycled on the Jumbovision screen: pretty girl, cute kid, old-timer, drunk fool. Your ubiquity comforted rather than irked. Your final notes made us switch the station in a frenzied search, and we'd catch your back end on the next button we tried. Through elaborate radio hopscotch, we could keep you with us the whole way home.

Your singer thought he had been discovered when he sang with last summer's voice. Before you were born, he bought his guitar secondhand from somebody's uncle, put those songs together in somebody's garage, wrote the lyrics on a napkin in somebody's bar. To him, the other songs on the album were every bit as charming as you. He was invited to sing you, the feel-good song of the summer, on late night talk shows. For the appearances, he messed up his hair, twitched unpredictably as he sang. He wanted to perform one of the experimental tracks off the album, but the host specifically requested he play you. The boys in the band talked him into assent. They knew what we knew: we didn't want experimental, we wanted the song that seemed to bring the sunshine with it, the only song that could do it for us, those three hot months.

The thirteen-year-olds misinterpreted their affection for you. You were puppy love, pure and sweet, a summer fling, not a foundation for hopes and futures. But they downloaded the whole album and bought the band's T-shirt, joined the fan club, tacked up the poster that would fall down in winter and never be raised again. The seventeen-year-olds, four years the wiser, knew better. Though they hung on every note, they could sense your mortality, imagine the limits of that voice and that sound, and realize it was not enough to sustain.

You are last summer's song, and you had the two-year-olds cooing and the teenagers shaking their hips, and middle-aged fingers hovering over the button when you came on, but relenting, letting you be. When we cheered you, the singer thought it was for him. The bass player knew better but kept that knowledge to himself. Your singer misconstrued our ageless affection for you as a universal fan base. They went on tour, the bass player and drummer enjoying themselves, basking in the residual glow. They loved you, played you enthusiastically, you: their milk and honey. The singer was annoyed. How had universal love boiled down to this: hordes of squealing thirteen-year-old girls? The singer pouted.

You were his creator more than he was yours, and he became your prodigal son.

He tired of playing you. His treatment of you became listless, then syncopated, then acoustic, and then toward the end of the tour, he refused to play you, utterly. Kept the crowds catching their breath, standing on toe tips, a hopeful clamor. Wanting to hear you the whole night: waiting, hungering, we the faithful who bought a ticket just to hear you live and loose and free, with imperfect instrumentals, fierce feedback, delicious distortion. We called for an encore that never came. We didn't speak as we rode home, we didn't listen to the radio. *They didn't play it,* was all we said to each other before retreating, troubled, to separate beds.

We bought you just to have you close, so we could play you when we needed to hear you. But you were a car song, a beach song, a roll-the-windows-down-and-throw-the-top-open song. We played you once, in the autumn, when the air was starting to crisp and the windows had to be shut against the chill and we had a touch of the good-bye-summer blues, we played you for cheer. But you belonged to the summer, reminded us of its passing, and hearing you made us more wistful yet. We put you aside.

Your singer has tried to put you behind him, and forget your past, but the rest of us never will; you were sunburned into us while we drove toward beaches and ball games. You supplied your singer with financial license to pursue his art. He recorded a second album in the winter, in which he restricted his voice to an affected, nasal falsetto. He fired the bass player and the lead guitarist quit, and so he was backed by only a bongo drummer and the occasional blast of a synthesized horn.

For some reason he is loved in Senegal, but we have forgotten him here.

The bass player became a carpenter in Montana, the lead guitarist became a Buddhist monk, the drummer bought a flower shop with his wife in Pasadena. The singer is in rehab, plotting his comeback. But the truth is, if he comes back, we will look the other way.

Your future is not bright. You will be placed on compilations of songs between other vaguely characteristic songs of your era, which will be sold through late night ads on local TV, for $19.95 plus shipping and handling, and tax, in Utah. On the commercials, struggling actors, dressed in poor imitations of the fashion of your time will attempt to dance to you, to affect the joy that we once felt when we heard you. But you belonged last summer, and when listening to you, so did we. When you are played on the radio now, you seem stale, lingering, an aged leading man with a defiant toupee, a lady nipped and tucked and tanned into a grotesquerie of youth.

It's time for a new infectious hook, a new pretty-boy face, a new theme for a new summer. And if you come on the radio we will change the station to quell the nausea. There is a new song now. Somewhere on tour in America, a bass player delivers his line, is buffeted by noisy crowd love, but knows better, and feels a dim sense of foreboding as the misdirected articles of clothing the girls toss gather about him, and he hands them, quietly, to the singer.

Hurts

Freshman year, Coach Sasser assigned Junebug, Isabel, and me to the junior varsity basketball team, where we wore the ill-fitting brown polyester uniforms of our high school, the Thomas Jefferson Spartans. On J.V., we were golden, thundering up and down the court with little form but much life. We threw up impossible shots and swatted away the attempts of pathetically shorter people and won games with scores like twenty to twelve. We hadn't met a play we didn't forget. We didn't know a foul we wouldn't commit. We couldn't learn a scam we wouldn't run. Isabel took off down the court before the other team even thought about shooting a basket, and when they bricked it, I'd grab the rebound and launch the ball. Junebug waited across the court, jumped to meet my pass, and had two or three chances to sink her lay-up before the other team, panting, caught up with her. *Cherry picking*, our rivals said, but we didn't care. A basket was a basket.

I was tall enough to be of use, quick enough to be in the right place at some of the right times, and accurate as any girl who played H.O.R.S.E. with her father on Saturday afternoons. Isabel was a steady point guard, a methodical dribbler, a careful passer, and a reluctant shooter.

Junebug had sauntered into the gym as a freshman shooting guard with a rep built in middle school. In a public district without organized ball until high school, this was not easy to do. She was loud, always letting out sounds with no meaning that she couldn't keep inside her. She passed with her mouth open, shot with her tongue out. She was a tiny, tawny lion, with baggy shorts down to her knees, striped socks raised to meet them, and an attitude that radiated from her. We were all taken in by her at first. She passed without looking and twisted, improbably, in mid-air. Junebug's moves were jazz made visible, until the ball, inevitably, clanged off the rim with a discrepant chord, or one of her beautiful but wild passes sent the ball flying to an unoccupied sideline.

"Can you make a lay-up?" Coach Sasser asked Junebug one day early in freshman season, standing on the sideline resplendent in her XL maroon tracksuit and mushroom-cap-shaped press-and-curl bob, her inch-long lacquered nails clutching the golden whistle that hung from a chain around her neck.

Junebug stood near the basket and bricked one stationary lay-up after another. We had to run a suicide for every one she missed. The next day we were sore. Before kids are big enough, they don't have enough force to make a basket anyway. Junebug had just looked good while trying, and that was enough for word to spread.

At the beginning of our sophomore season, Junebug, Isabel, and I made the varsity basketball team, and we thought we would be playing side by side, every once in a while at least, when the starters needed rest.

Instead, we sat the bench. That was how we said it—we didn't sit *on* the bench, we *sat the bench,* as if it were a part of us, as if we had mutated to meld with it. We hadn't expected it to be that way. Our J.V. record was immaculate, though the games themselves were a stain. We were happy enough at first, just to wear matching uniforms that didn't encase us like sausages the way the J.V. ones had, happy enough to run out with the team and see our names in the program, even if they were misspelled. But as the first game passed without us touching the court, then another, and another, we wanted to play with an intensity that unmoored us.

Not that we deserved to play at first. Charmaine Grand, the senior starting point guard, grew up playing street ball with the boys and now she dazzled with her skills. If we had been put in, bringing our rowdy ostentation, we would have looked like fools next to Charmaine's quiet grace. She was slim and muscled and her hands could do clever things with the ball that we'd have to watch in slow motion to fully understand. When we ran wind sprints, Junebug was the only one who came anywhere close to matching Charmaine's speed.

We slogged through school days, listless with deprivation from playing time, turning on our energy only for the afternoon practices that could earn us a chance to play. Classes were a haze of daydreams in which I was invited on a court that opened up before me, a streak of sunlight cutting the way to the basket. If Coach Sasser put me in on varsity, who's to say I wouldn't just dunk that ball?

Junebug, my chemistry lab partner, interrupted my reverie to talk about people who actually played. "Nico, did you see that pass Charmaine made in the scrimmage yesterday? She was looking one way and the ball went the other." Junebug held her goggles away from her face when she wasn't mixing chemicals so she wouldn't get the cheek dents that would brand her as a science nerd as we emerged from the lab.

"What about that blind backdoor lay-up she made?" I adjusted the titration apparatus. "And her hair is so—" I sought the word, "shiny."

Junebug shook her head once, sharp. I knew what this meant: *please stop talking so we can still be friends.*

I thought about Charmaine's hair: glossy chin-length black curls. Many of my teammates struggled to settle on a hairdo that would endure all the sweating we did. Braids were a practical option but weren't in fashion at the moment. Junebug wore her hair in a cute high ponytail that curved precisely under like a fat apostrophe. I knew she protected it at night with a bandana because once she'd shown up for an early Saturday practice with this granny kerchief still on. My own lank hair, the color of a brown mouse pelt, looked equally bad sweaty or dry. I had a cowlick in front that parted my bangs down the middle, no matter how I tried to join them. Charmaine's hair wasn't just shiny. It glistened. It was a Jheri Curl, powered by activator. As a white girl, I struggled with Black hair math, but I finally put it together that this far into the '90s, this style wasn't allowed. None of my classmates had dripped Jheri Curl juice on my math papers, dotting them with translucent spots, since middle school. So that's why Junebug hushed me. I'd discovered our hero's Achilles' heel. Charmaine had found a hairdo that worked and held onto it for too long.

"What the hell is everyone doing without their goggles on?" our chemistry teacher shouted. Junebug and I were the only ones with our goggles pushed up just then, but to him it looked like mutiny. We readjusted their goggles and scuttled back to our station.

"Any dents?" she asked, that day as always, before we parted.

"No dents," I said.

That afternoon when the principal brought in a Thomas Jefferson impersonator for an all-school assembly it caused a near riot. Although the speaker's attire was the subject of plenty of cracks, most people listened while the wig-wearing man in breeches and hose clomped around the stage in his colonial shoes, delivering a boring speech about Monticello and founding the country. At the end students were allowed to question the great man, and Junebug shot her hand up to ask the first one, "Why did you own slaves?"

As Jefferson began to answer, kids rose from their seats and heckled, hooting and throwing balled-up paper. The principal took the mic to quiet us down, made us listen to the impersonator's answer, and then asked for another question. Jefferson called on a junior in the front, ignoring the frantic way the principal was shaking his head. "How many times did you have sex with your slaves?" the kid boomed.

The crowd roared, everyone leaping out of their seats. The principal should have known better. The only assemblies where everybody paid respectful attention were those that featured the members of Brother to Brother performing a dazzling, coordinated step routine in their matching buff Timberlands, their unified stomps echoing off the gym floor. The principal ushered the impersonator out to the wings of the stage under a hail of thrown paper.

At practice, we tried to make ourselves feel a part of the team, participating in the sideline gossip sessions while waiting our turn in drills.

"What's our non-district game this year?" Junebug asked Reggie, a six-foot tall junior.

"Pinnacle Christian," Reggie said. She paused, put her hands on her hips, assessed the progress of the drill. "I heard they're racist," she added.

"Who said?" I asked.

"My cousin—she plays for 'Bello." Reggie glanced at Sasser to make sure she wouldn't launch a basketball at our faces for looking the wrong way. "She said the Pinnacle team used some ugly words when they played them."

"Who doesn't use ugly words when they play Montbello?" I said, but no one laughed.

"Mountain girls never see anything but white people their whole lives," Junebug said.

"Something like that," Reggie said, shrugging her shoulders.

Junebug puffed herself up, spanked the basketball she held in her hands, and shouted, too loud, "We've got to beat that ass."

Coach Sasser blew the whistle. "Since you can't pay attention, you might as well get on the line." I wondered if she'd promoted us to varsity just to prompt extra running drills to punish our mistakes.

We swore, collectively, under our breath as we approached the baseline that was our sprinting starting mark. During the rest of the practice, the story passed in fragments, and was embellished, falsified. Reggie said the Pinnacle coach told the Montbello coach "*You people* can use the guest locker room." Althea, the center, a solid brick of a girl who protected her recently-aligned teeth with a terrifying red mouthpiece, said she'd heard a Pinnacle fan assumed one of the girl's mothers was a janitor and pointed out a spilled soda to her. One Pinnacle player had told a Montbello player, "Your hair smells like baby puke." At the end of it, I didn't know whose cousin was the subject of this abuse. Maybe she was a cousin to all of us, after that, even the four of us known on the team as "the white girls": me, a dishwater blonde Warrant-aficionado named Joli, Isabel, whose mom was from El Salvador, and Laura, a junior guard who was adopted from Vietnam.

Charmaine took no part in gossip. While we talked, our voices and gestures becoming animated with anger, she stood three paces off, working on her dribbling. She directed the ball between her legs and around in a fluid motion, keeping her eyes on the back wall.

It was the same way every season, when the same old rumors washed down from the mountains to the city. In Denver, we played each of the other nine teams in the district twice and one or two out-of-conference games each season. We played one across-state team, and always someone on our team had a cousin or a niece or an aunt on another who had played them already and brought away a dark report. It motivated us to cast our opponent in that evil light and make whatever we accomplished on the court into a crusade against small-town backwardness.

That was when the games became more about honor than basketball, and life on the bench grew more agitated. The first big game that season was at hoops powerhouse Montbello, a tract in northernmost Denver where the mountain view is blocked by industry and HUD houses spring up in birthday cake colors: lavender trimmed with violet, baby blue with Pepto Bismol pink, bubblegum with magenta. In Montbello, keeping the color of house paint within reason is the least of people's worries. Montbello was an enemy that we understood, a high school like ours where it was possible to graduate without being taught how to read, filled with kids who were the reasons other parents sent their own to private school.

We hated the girls on the Montbello team like sisters, and our violence toward each other was of the hair-pulling and name-calling variety. "Montghetto," we called them, and wondered what they called us. But we never feared them, never feared what we felt toward them. We just wanted to meet them on the court and win.

The game was fierce and sloppy. The teams played with a degree of intensity usually reserved for when the stands were at least a quarter full. But as usual, the game took place before the company of an odd assortment of loafing janitors and the strange old man who came to every afternoon girls' game wearing the same pair of gray pants and watched us while he did the crossword puzzle and drank canned tea.

Junebug, Isabel, and I fought to position ourselves on either side of Coach Sasser, hoping that her eyes would stray on us and that would give her an idea. We could smell her gardenia perfume, and out of the corner of our eyes catch a glimpse of the silk scarf that was always at her throat during games, complementing her pantsuit, the scarf of a color that a woman couldn't wear until she was of a certain age: mustard, taupe, tangerine. We monitored our periphery for any signs of the scarf's movement that might indicate she was about to make a change. We sat on the edges of our seats, leaned our elbows on our knees, and clasped our hands together in an attitude of prayer. The game was close, the lead see-sawing back and forth. When Coach met our eyes, she looked away quickly, uncomfortable with our hunger. By fourth quarter, we had been pushed out to the edges, as Coach Sasser squeezed replacements next to her for quick instructions. On the bench, we parched ourselves with longing, drinking dry the water bottles that were meant for those who played.

Our team was up by eight with two minutes left on the clock. The Montbello fans tried to rattle us, starting up a chant:

He-ey, number 3-4,

your greasy curl's dripping on our floor!

I looked at Junebug and Isabel in disbelief. Charmaine wore 34. Junebug bit down hard on the hand towels we were given to wipe up sweat—though ours were merely decorative—to keep from screaming. "Put me in, put me in," she chanted under her breath.

But Charmaine didn't need our help. The chant stopped when she busted two three-pointers in a row, putting the game out of reach for Montbello.

After the buzzer sounded, we went out to center court to slap the starters' hands, Junebug and I struggling to keep up smiles that were something like sincere. We didn't speak during the long bus ride home, and didn't sleep that night. I never slept after games. Having had no practice to wear me out, my body was stretched and primed in warm-up but my heart was never allowed to pump quick and my sweat was not permitted to flow. I kicked at the sheets. I cocooned myself in them. I squeezed my eyes tight to keep out invasive beams of moonlight that seemed to enter through the window with intent to taunt. All night I thought about what I'd have done if I'd been put in against Montbello, imagining myself hitting a fadeaway jumper that would impress Coach Sasser and Charmaine.

I greeted Junebug in chemistry the next morning, her expression a sullen mirror of my own, and we sat like two grim zombies, thinking about the next game in which we'd wait and wait for a call to play that would never come.

A person made to wait too long goes one of two ways. Some of them get mean, like they've been beaten at random so long that they see each new day as a stick raised to strike. The others develop the patience of saints. Junebug got mean. She kicked things. She kicked a locker so hard she broke her little toe. But she didn't quit practicing and she didn't quit running. She told no one she was injuring herself from practicing so hard, but I guessed at her winces and secretive limps. At practice, she turned her pain to such rage as to wither grape to raisin at a glance. Isabel was the saintly one, offering cool bottles of water and new towels to the starters as they came off the court. "You deserve to play," she told Junebug and me after every game that passed without a chance to break a sweat.

The three of us benchies practiced harder than the complacent starters. We practiced so hard, we snapped things and pulled things and sprained things and tore things. And we never said a word, because any injury put us further from getting in the game. Even when healed, the residue of past injury imprinted on Coach Sasser's brain could lead her to ration our playing time. We didn't even compare aches with each other, as we used to on J.V. We just let out furtive little moans, now and then, to keep each other informed. We didn't go out on weekends. We spent them alternately icing and heating parts of our bodies, and our sheets smelled of Ben Gay and Flex-All. The fumes made us irritable.

"Damn this stuff is funky," Junebug would say when we gathered fragrantly at someone's house to catch a movie. Then she'd threaten: "I'm switching to Red Hot." But Red Hot, the subtle-scented wonder, seemed to be available only on the coaches' black market. There was an unmarked, crimson jar of it in Coach Sasser's training bag, and if we used it, she would know.

One day after practice, Charmaine stopped me as I was leaving the locker room. "I have something for you three." She plopped her bag down on a bench and rummaged through it. Junebug and Isabel arrived next to me instantly, Junebug craning her neck to see what Charmaine was digging for.

"Here," Charmaine said, handing us clear jar of Red Hot, the glowing liniment inside the color of chili powder. We hadn't asked for it, but she knew. "You ladies keep on," she said.

I hesitated to take it, but Junebug snatched it out of her hand. "Praise Jesus," Junebug said, and Charmaine laughed. It was Charmaine who had named her Junebug, nonchalantly, at a pre-season pick-up game, before she learned her proper name. Who knew what it meant. The word had left Charmaine's mouth and we abided by it. Junebug wore her nickname like a medal, grinned to hear it called, glad not to have to answer anymore to Geraldine.

We didn't know how to share custody of the Red Hot so we waited until everyone left the locker room and applied it.

"My ankle," I moaned, letting out what I'd been holding in all season.

"My hamstring," Junebug said.

"I pulled something in my butt," Isabel said.

"Here," Junebug said, handing her the jar. "You put this on in privacy. But bring it back. It's coming home with me tonight."

The week before the Pinnacle Christian game, practices were solemn affairs where Coach Sasser, nervous, tried to teach us new plays. We'd learn seven or eight variations on each play, but we never used them. The best the starters did was set up in the play formation and pass the ball around a bit before succumbing to their impulses toward chaos and throwing up whatever would go. It was different before district games, when we'd talk about the girls we were going to play, giving them names if we didn't know them.

"I can take Broccoli Head," I always claimed before we played Kennedy. Broccoli Head wore a wide, tight headband and her thick hair puffed out of it like the top of her vegetable namesake.

But Pinnacle preparation practices were silent. We didn't know the girls and we didn't name them. We didn't need a label to understand what they were to us.

We were allowed to leave school before last period to begin the bus ride to Pinnacle, out of the city, up into the mountains. Before it was time to warm up in their bright, clean gym, a fringe of blue mountains visible through the high windows, we observed the Pinnacle team like anthropologists. They were big and blond, as the mountain teams were every year. They wore matching white Nike high-tops and red uniforms with expensive appliqued numbers—ours were silk-screened and our shoes were whatever our moms could find at Payless. They all seemed to be between five-nine and six-one, with the exception of the one requisite, feisty little point guard.

This year, it was Isabel's turn to say: "They grow 'em big in the mountains."

We were calm at first. It was the warm-up music that did us in. Over the tinny loudspeaker, they piped an uneasy mixture of early-'80s New Edition and Run DMC.

"Oh Lord," Junebug said. "Just because we've got Black people on our team, they have to go and dig out the old school stuff. They can't find anything newer than this? How long's it take for songs to reach the mountains?"

"Hey," Reggie shouted at them across the court. "You ladies still watching the Dukes of Hazard?"

They laughed cheerily, as if it were a joke to be shared. We're all friends, right? Spunky Little Point Guard smiled.

We clowned through "Cool it Now," missing our lay-ups from lack of care until Coach Sasser yelled at us. At home games, we warmed up to Marvin Gaye, at Coach's insistence. If you could sink free throws while listening to "Sexual Healing," the theory ran, you could sink them under any condition.

Our cheerleaders had come with us, thinking we'd need support, and it was comforting to have them there, substantial women with powerful thighs who made their voices artificially deep as they barked out cheers. The Thomas Jefferson cheerleaders made the Pinnacle ones, who tinkled around, exclaiming in their high-pitched voices, look insignificant. Which was helpful, because the Pinnacle stands brimmed with fans, while ours held only Gramps and his can of tea.

I looked over at the Pinnacle team during warm-up, trying to hide my glances. It was their free throws that began to frighten me.

Toe the line. Dribble three times. Crouch. Breathe. Extend. Release. Swish. It was clear they practiced with their eyes closed. In Denver Public Schools games, any free throw you happened to make was considered a bonus. They dribbled like they had practiced their precision around orange cones for years and moved in their plays like studying their playbook came before homework. They looked like they had searched themselves over for spots of weakness and honed. When the coach called them, they ran toward him as a unit, their golden ponytails swinging together like bright bells on Christmas morning. It was more than just basketball, though. In the way they walked, you could see that they knew what a gerund was and how to use it, and how to diagram a sentence and conjugate a verb in French and ride a horse and play the piano. They couldn't relate to us well enough to perceive which of us had unacceptable hairstyles. Their extended families filled the stands, wearing their school colors and buttons with pictures of them that said "My All Star."

At the tip-off I was glad for once that I wasn't in, nervous to test my swarthy city self against the wholesome mountain version of a white girl that I could never live up to. But as the game wore on, I wanted to play again, worse than ever. Pinnacle ran plays with names and numbers, all a boring variation on their school colors. The point would bring the ball up the court, pause while they organized themselves, shout "Crimson" or "Gold" or "White," hold up a quantity of fingers, and set the play in motion. When our team got the ball, we acted like half-starved guests at a banquet who didn't have the sense to take the turkey slow so not to choke. Joli launched the ball to Charmaine at mid-court, who dribbled down and passed it to Reggie at post. By this time the Pinnacle girls had already set up their careful zone defense, and our team would pass the ball back and forth to each other helplessly until one of them got anxious and tried to drive to the hoop, where they were inevitably rejected by one of Pinnacle's huge baseline guardians.

It wasn't long before our team began to play thug ball. We entered that gym thinking they looked down on us, and we soon began to behave so that they did. You can only put up with a snotty zone defense and time-wasting plays for so long until the need to foul rises up within you and moves your limbs to action. With slaps and steals and scrappy defense, our team tried to claw their way back. And half of them fouled out doing it. Althea hit five by driving an elbow into the Pinnacle center's stomach. She accompanied the move with an alarming roar. In the third quarter Reggie clotheslined the low post. In the fourth quarter, Joli lost control of herself and smacked the point guard right across her cheeky little face.

A whistle blew. "We don't play that way here, young lady," the ref informed her.

Joli rolled her eyes, curled her lip. She had five anyway. When someone fouled out, the refs gave the coach a little time to figure out what to do next. Joli walked under the basket and Coach Sasser stood up to talk to her. Coach turned around and surveyed us leftovers on the bench. She had the look of a person who wanted to close the refrigerator door, pray a little, and try again. If we had been any farther on the edge of our seats, we would have fallen off.

"Uhh," Coach said. Somewhere in the stands, a child cried out. A cheerleader rustled her pompom. Gramps sneezed. "Nico," Coach decided.

Isabel turned her bright eyes toward me and smiled. Junebug kept her hard look trained forward. I felt like a traitor to them, but I leapt up like I'd sat on something sharp.

Coach put her hand on my shoulder. "Go in there, and guard 52. If you get the ball, take your time. Wait for your shot. Or pass it. Okay?"

I nodded like a puppy. I trotted out on the court and tried to get my bearings. Charmaine gestured to me. "Remember, that basket is ours," she said, pointing.

The whistle blew. I was a rusty spring wound up for too many weeks, and I sprung out madly. My five minutes of play was a fiasco of missed and misdirected passes, over-eager and sloppy and shameful. My inability to control myself frustrated me, so I did the only thing I could do. When I got a rebound, I swung my elbows like a scythe.

In the larger world, violence may solve nothing, but on the basketball court, it at least relieves.

I went up, swinging my elbows for a rebound, and came down with a Pinnacle girl's fingernail in my eye. The ref called a foul. The girl had ripped my contact out and scraped a patch of skin off my cheek so I approached the free throw line with half-blurred vision. I made the first one, which was something I couldn't do with regular sight. I guess shooting at the basket in the middle of the three made more sense. I didn't tell anyone that she had cut me. I didn't want to leave. But blood started to seep from the scrape under my eye. I bricked the second one and Coach set me down, she replaced me, she returned me, hurting, to the bench. On my way out, Junebug, who was subbing in for me, looked at me and it fueled her rage. "A mountain girl jacked Nico's eyeball!" she announced. She conferenced with the more thuggish individuals on our team surreptitiously, while Charmaine tried to reign, tried to maintain dignity. There was no dignity left to be had.

If you closed your eyes and listened to the last few minutes of that game, you would hear cheap slaps and nail scrapes and the dull thuds of elbows driving into unprepared flesh. If you closed them tight so you could listen with the intensity of the blind, you could hear the bruises forming, the platelets gathering under sweat-beaded skin, you could hear the welts beginning to rise.

The score was an albatross, a rotting weight to wear all season, a loss of sixty to twenty-three. The whole maddening carnival of Pinnacle Christian relatives jeered at us as we headed out the gym. This time no one mistook it for racism but saw it for what it was: color-blind hate. Coach Sasser said just one thing to us as we walked to the bus: "Don't hang your heads, ladies, but keep them lifted." We all knew the next day she would run us until we puked.

On the bus, we grabbed solitary seats. I pressed my cheek to the cool, dirty windowpane, put my hand to my throbbing eye, and swallowed my hurts. We wouldn't talk about them, that night or ever. Later my dad would take me to the emergency room to check on the red, crescent-shaped cut in the white of my eye. I worried they'd make me wear an eye patch and I'd be benched for the rest of the season. But when the doctor just wrote me a prescription for antibiotic eyedrops, I wished I had some more visible symbol of how badly I'd wanted to play, how readily I would sacrifice my body for another chance at it. At the pharmacy as we waited for my eyedrops, I found a black cloth eye patch and asked my dad if he'd buy it. "Twenty dollars?" he said and whistled. "Let's go home."

Local Honey

In the bathroom at the Wu-Tang Clan concert, Gwen read this message on the hand dryer as she steeled herself to reenter the stuffy, thumping auditorium outside: *For your well-being we have installed electric hand dryers to protect you against the dangers of disease that may be transmitted by cloth towels or paper towel litter. Medical tests prove that electric drying minimizes the possibilities of disease.* Gwen wished she could wear such a plaque, front and center, defending her family's existence so people wouldn't wonder and wouldn't stare. *For our well-being my husband and I adopted a child. We are white, our son is Black. Sociological studies prove this child-rearing arrangement can work out as well others, so don't worry about us.*

Gwen and Steven Overby ceded control of the car radio to their son Hugh when he turned twelve. Instead of the Boulder community radio station's African Roots or Bluegrass Breakfast shows, Hugh chose the Denver hip-hop station. To Gwen, the DJs on it always seemed to be shouting, as if they were in a crowded club, trying to make themselves heard over the din. The people in the commercials spoke in affected street-smart accents, often above a background of sirens and other raucous sound effects.

Gwen tolerated the station and still hoped this music would grow on her, because she was reluctant to become the sort of parent who would detest her child's music. She often thought about something she'd read in the pamphlets the adoption counselor pressed on her long ago: occasionally adult interracial adoptees moved far away, settled into a community of their own race and denied their adoptive parents. Would he do that to them, their Hugh? She hoped learning to enjoy Hugh's favorite music would be one small way to prevent this.

It was Gwen who heard the DJ announce that the Wu-Tang Clan would perform in Denver soon after Hugh's fourteenth birthday, and it was Gwen who observed how Hugh turned the radio up when the DJ said this, how he leaned forward and stared into it as if he could glean more information by scrutinizing the number on the display. And it was Gwen who helped hang the posters of the Wu-Tang Clan that papered her son's walls, and let him use her credit card to download the Wu-Tang Clan's music.

Despite this, Gwen would later claim that it had been Steven's idea to accompany their son to the Wu-Tang concert. But they wouldn't be able to begin their argument about the genesis of this plan until after they endured the show, pushed through the crowd to the exit, drove home to Boulder and lay sleepless on their pillows, temples pounding to separate rhythms. Had they known anything about it, they would have tried something lighter first, like the Black Eyed Peas or The Roots. Had they known anything about it, they would have brought earplugs and worn steel-toed boots. Had they known anything about it, they would have realized that their attempt at bonding with Hugh would in fact accelerate his de-bonding from them that began the day he started kindergarten.

When Hugh opened his birthday card and three tickets to the concert fell out, he beamed. Then Steven said, "I thought we could all go together."

"We?" Hugh asked.

"Yeah—me, you, and Mom."

Hugh's expression betrayed the tug of two contrary emotions. "Do you like the Wu-Tang Clan?" he asked, cautiously.

"Well, I haven't made up my mind about them yet," Steven said. "But I know they're your favorite, so we wanted to give them a try."

"Oh," Hugh said. "But can't I take Isaac and Cecil?"

"You have to be sixteen to go without a parent," Steven said.

"We went to a few concerts in our day," Gwen added. "I don't remember why we ever stopped going."

Gwen and Steven mentioned the concert more often during the week leading up to it than Hugh did. "Are you ready for the big show?" Steven would ask every night before Hugh retreated to his bedroom. Hugh would shrug and smile, and say, "Night Mom, night Dad." Gwen wondered if they were doing the right thing.

One day that week Gwen noticed her family reflected in the mirrored windows of a building that they were approaching and didn't recognize them for a moment. Who were these stooped, washed-out people with lank gray hair, looking every bit of their fifty-two years, wearing drab earth-toned T-shirts and faded denim, and what was this bright young man doing with them? Hugh was tall and striking, in dark indigo jeans and a crisp shirt so yellow that it taught those who beheld it what that color should be. He looked like a volunteer in some rehabilitation program that paired vital youths with burnt-out hippies. Just why, after all, had she stopped updating the frames of her glasses some time during the waning Bush administration? Why had she let Steven convince her to take advantage of the vision plan they had then by purchasing three identical pairs of a rather too large, tortoiseshell frame that she had once liked? She wondered how long she had been committing these crimes of style, and how Hugh had developed his own sense of fashion without her to guide him.

What she remembered best from the time before they adopted Hugh was the summers, the marvelous Colorado summers that began in May and stretched through September. Gwen and Steven wore loose clothes made of natural fibers and drank homebrewed beer and picnicked in the mountains. They had jobs, of course, but Gwen could hardly remember spending much time at them. All of their friends and everyone in Boulder, it seemed, were having babies, the women swelling as the days grew hotter, and then another one would arrive, and eventually join the others toddling through the grass. Babies tumbled around at the summer parties where always some man strummed a guitar and everyone sipped tea brewed from the leaves of many nations, sweetened with local honey.

Gwen and Steven wanted a baby too. They tried on the hilltops, groping each other on a blanket over ground full of red sandstones that jabbed them. They tried in the high valleys amid biting insects that buzzed among the aster and the Indian paintbrush. They tried under shelter during the brief afternoon thunderstorms that rolled in from the mountains. They tried in the early morning and the dark of night. Outdoor sex was uncomfortable and required more craft than the indoor variety, but they wanted to invite all the forces of nature to bring them a healthy child.

Gwen and Steven didn't understand why they couldn't make a baby. They lived fertile lives. They slept naked and ate food from the farmers' market. They grew basil, kohlrabi, and zucchini in the unpromising rocky dirt of their backyard easily enough. They went to doctors to discuss fertility treatments, but the methods that science offered to aid conception seemed unnatural, and being natural was the whole point for them back then. Neither could remember which of them first suggested the idea of adoption, but they both took to it right away. This was the better way, participating in a natural scenario, one set of parents picking up where another left off.

The adoption counselor, a woman with steel-gray pin curls and a severe expression who wore cushy, brandless black sneakers, told them the wait could stretch on for years. They asked the counselor to explain their options. As she spoke, Gwen realized the cruel hierarchy of adoption. At the apex lolled the Healthy White Infant, guaranteed love, passed from God through a woman to his rightful parents, his transition from one family to another as simple and elegant as world-class sprinters passing a baton. Then came the others: Romanian toddlers, Chinese girls, adolescent and elementary school-aged foster kids. Then the crack babies and kids with disabilities and health problems. But Gwen and Steven didn't have to agree to this ranking of worth.

Gwen and Steven turned toward each other and met eyes. They thought: Of course. We don't need a white one. If they insisted on a white infant with no health concerns, they would wait for years. "We will welcome any child," Gwen said, "Though we would like a baby, if possible." Gwen had always loved babies—their gummy smiles, their sweet, soft heads.

"The wait is longer if you want a light-skinned child," the counselor said.

Gwen looked at the counselor in horror at this concept. "We don't care," Gwen said, offended that the counselor might have thought they did. "What do you do, line the kids up and compare their skin color to a paper bag?"

The counselor leaned forward. "I'm not asking this for your benefit. I'm screening the kids from prospective parents who want the option to sample and return."

"That's not us," Gwen said. She felt she had been waiting all her life, patiently at times, restlessly at others, and her desire for a child had begun as a low hum, then became a buzz, and grew louder until it now it was keening, and she couldn't wait one moment longer. Bring her a child as dark as she was pale, as uniform in skin tone as she was freckled, and she would dare anyone to say that it wasn't her right to mother him.

Hugh came to them at age three months, with asthma and congenital hip dysplasia that would one day require surgery. He was a good baby, and at five months he slept through the night. Gwen's friends sometimes complained about their babies' constant clinging, the way their babies grabbed their hair and earrings, marked their clothes with territorial spit, sucked their nipples raw, and woke them in the night, but Gwen wanted Hugh close. She relished it. She loved attending to his every fuss, tickling his feet, rubbing his skin with cocoa butter until he shone like a glossy tropical nut.

In the years after the Overbys adopted Hugh, psychologists began to investigate the effects of white couples raising Black children. Gwen read the results of the studies in adoption newsletters. Most concluded that the kids did best when they lived in integrated neighborhoods and went to school with other Black children. When Hugh was little, it never occurred to the Overbys that they were making more than the usual missteps as parents, and they never considered leaving Boulder, whose population was eighty percent white and less than one percent Black. Gwen could practically name all the Black people in Boulder, such as the Africans who taught at the world dance and drumming school, a handful of students, and the street performer who could fold himself to fit inside a small plexiglass box. Boulder was a beautiful town that transitory people often tarried in for a time, and many of them became stuck, as the Overbys had, with good jobs and stellar public schools for Hugh to attend.

Besides, Hugh was immediately popular at school, a five-year-old invited to so many birthday parties that Steven fretted over the cost of the presents. Hugh learned and grew and made friends and developed a disposition so sunny that depressed people turned to him like flowers toward the light. Steven taught his son how to telemark ski and fish for rainbow trout in the mountain streams. He taught Hugh how to set up camp, how to focus a telescope and read a compass, a GPS, and a topographic map. He told Hugh to make a fist, drew concentric circles around Hugh's knuckle, then had him stretch his hand out to demonstrate what mountains looked like in flat representation.

Gwen read Hugh a story before he went to bed every night and stirred a spoonful of local honey into his cereal each morning because she had read that it prevented the development of pollen allergies. When he was scared of the dark she taught him a prayer from her childhood, though she hadn't said it in years. They bought him biographies of prominent African Americans and forced him to watch *Roots* and *Eyes on The Prize* with them. They attended bimonthly meetings of Families of Interracial Adoptees, but most of the other kids were from China or Guatemala, most of the children were girls, and most of them were much younger than Hugh.

But everyone in town was welcoming of the Overbys. It was only when the Overbys left Boulder that strangers would look at them, glance away, and then look again. Once at a restaurant when they were driving out to the eastern plains to see Steven's family, the hostess started to seat Gwen and Steven separately from Hugh. "Table for three, not two," Gwen had corrected the hostess, who apologized and hustled away from them as quickly as she could. Often strangers looking at them didn't even perceive them as a unit, as a family.

When Hugh was twelve, he and Gwen were walking through the mall in Denver, and they passed a group of Black teenagers. Hugh fell silent, but Gwen kept talking. "Now, do you need new jeans for school? You're growing so fast these days. Probably should get some socks and underwear, too." Hugh didn't respond, and Gwen glanced at the boys, who were grinning, listening carefully to their conversation, trying to figure out what the joke was, trying to determine why Hugh was following some white lady around the mall. Hugh pivoted and headed for the exit. "Hugh!" Gwen called. "Where are you going? I need to stop at Walgreens." Then the boys began to cackle, and Hugh quickened his pace, hurrying away from her. When she rushed out to find him and ask him what was the matter, he wouldn't say, he just kept repeating, "Let's go home, Mom, let's go home now."

At thirteen Hugh began to grow relentlessly, and being close to him felt like standing near a source of pulsating energy, a barely contained force ready to break out and assert itself. He ate voraciously and seemed to radiate heat. His emotions became palpable in any room he occupied, whether he expressed them or not. Gwen could sense anger, in particular, when he asked her advice on his Algebra homework and she misread a story problem. When he was halfway through working it the way she suggested, she would correct herself and instruct him to do it a different way. Hugh would silently seethe for a moment before he began to erase what he had written, so violently that sometimes the paper tore. One afternoon Hugh came into the kitchen while Gwen was making carob chip cookies with honey, and he exploded at her. "I'm sick of honey!" he shouted. "Normal people use sugar. The white kind, not that brown health crap. SHU-GERRR. And carob tastes nothing like chocolate. Carob tastes like ass."

Gwen phoned the counselor who had helped them with the adoption to ask what was happening to Hugh, what was becoming of her open, inquisitive, happy child? The counselor ventured that the behavior she described was normal for a teenager, but suggested that she try to offer him more opportunities to socialize with Black people of his age or older. Gwen considered signing Hugh up for a YMCA basketball league in Denver, but worried about the traffic and construction they would contend with driving to the games. Gwen failed to convince Hugh that it would be a good idea to take an African dance class from the Ghanaian gentleman who strode the town in his dashiki. The Overbys began making weekend excursions to Denver, where Hugh could at least see more Black people, but Gwen didn't know if this was helping.

On the evening of the concert, the Overbys departed early, but when they arrived at the Fillmore, the line stretched from the security guards' blockade by the doors down the sidewalk for two blocks. It was an immense, shambling, disorganized line. The people waiting to see the show had to be teenagers, but they looked much younger to Gwen. There was a busy police station directly across the street, and still people smoked weed. Hugh stood stiffly, facing forward in line, gradually inching away from his parents while Gwen and Steven debated from which direction the pot they smelled was coming, engaging in a conversation they once would have mocked.

They finally reached the security station and presented themselves for a pat-down, and Gwen's purse didn't pass inspection. The security worker held up a metal nail file and said, "Sorry, ma'am, you can't bring this in." Gwen stared at him. "You could shank someone with this," the guard explained. Before Gwen had processed this information, Hugh declared, "I'll wait for you guys inside," and ducked through the doors. When Gwen returned from depositing the objectionable item in the car, she found Steven standing just inside the doors, where they had agreed to meet, but Hugh was nowhere in sight.

"He wanted to take a closer look, and this is close enough for me," Steven said, "So I let him go ahead. There aren't even any seats. What kind of theater doesn't have any seats?"

Gwen scanned the crowd. "You know," she said, "It's mostly white kids here."

"Did you think that all the Black people in Denver would turn out because it's a rap show?"

"No," Gwen said. But she had been thinking something like that.

Gwen and Steven were the oldest people in the Fillmore, even older than most of the bartenders and bouncers. But it was clear that no one noticed them. The concertgoers were too taken with their own youth, vitality, and search for illicit substances to perceive them standing in the back of the packed theater.

"Hugh is growing up," Steven observed. "He never wants to get up early on the weekends like he used to, and spend the day outside with me."

It was the first time Steven had acknowledged to Gwen that his relationship with Hugh was shifting. "Maybe Hugh doesn't want to go hiking every weekend anymore," Gwen said. "Maybe his interests have changed."

"Well, maybe Hugh doesn't want to help bake organic pita bread for your women's group anymore, and then sit around listening to them yammer incessantly about their dogs like no one ever had a dog before."

Gwen looked at her husband. "I never realized how ridiculous you found me," she said. Steven was right about her friends, particularly Lydia, who would often tell a story about her dog and then turn toward the dog and repeat it to him in a high-pitched voice, presumably to aid the animal's comprehension. Gwen wanted to do something Steven wouldn't expect. "I'm going in."

"You're crazy. I'm staying back here."

"Suit yourself." Gwen turned and walked into the crowd alone. She couldn't see anything from her vantage on the main floor, so she climbed the stairs to the balcony on the side of the stage for a better view. She found an open space along the front railing and began to search the crowd for Hugh. She saw her husband, standing where she left him, his arms crossed over his chest, shifting his weight from side to side and fuming at having been left alone. Then she spotted Hugh, who pushed his way forward among the increasingly restless crowd, weaving in and out, detecting and aiming for each gap that appeared until he had worked his way toward the front. The crowd repelled groups and pairs of people who were attempting similar maneuvers, as the people near the stage jockeyed to maintain their positions and the ones toward the back clamored to overtake them, but everyone let a loner pass.

Just as Hugh was about to breach the packed space within a fifteen-foot radius of the stage, a woman squeezed in next to Gwen, jostling her and making her lose track of Hugh. "Quit hogging this good view," the woman said. "I drove all the way from Pueblo and I had to beg my sister to watch my kids. I'm not going to miss anything." The woman looked barely out of her teens, wore thick black eyeliner, and had a Wu-Tang tattoo on her bared shoulder, a sharp, angry W that resembled a deformed bat.

Gwen nodded and smiled weakly, but then the house lights dimmed, the Wu-Tang Clan burst from backstage, the music started, and the woman went absolutely insane, grinding her hips in a roving semicircle and flailing her arms, repeatedly smacking Gwen in the glasses, trying to bump her back from the balcony. Gwen gripped the railing and attempted to maintain her space so she could watch Hugh.

Gwen had never experienced such bass before, emanating from demonic speakers stacked to the rafters, pounding in her chest so hard her heartbeat was obscured. Gwen could sense the damage she was doing to her hearing and believed she could pinpoint the precise moment each of the cilia in her inner ear trembled and was lost. The members of the Wu-Tang Clan kept emerging from and retreating into the wings, strutting back and forth across the stage, pumping their arms, never standing still or remaining assembled long enough for Gwen to make an accurate count of them. Every time a new one appeared, the crowd's already seismic roar increased, and it seemed to Gwen that each successive member was somehow even more famous and beloved than the last. Whenever Gwen thought she had gained a fix on Hugh, the woman would slam into her with her hip, disguising the assault as a dance move. It was tiring to sustain her position in the face of this onslaught, and about mid-way through the fifth song, Gwen gave up and retreated to the bathroom. The moment Gwen vacated her spot the woman assumed it, raising her arms aloft and throwing up the same pro-Wu-Tang hand gestures that others in the crowd were making.

Gwen spent a long time in the bathroom, staring at the puddles and soaked, wadded fluorescent ads for various clubs that littered the counter around the sinks and reading and rereading the plaque on the hand dryer. *For your well-being*, it began, and continued in such a confident and reassuring tone that Gwen hoped to derive some useful message from it. If she were to install such a hand dryer at home, would it improve her life the way it promised to improve a bathroom, rendering it proper, neat, and orderly? Could it calm her burgeoning son back into his pleasant childhood temperament, could it make her husband more expressive and less self-involved? Gwen compared the bathroom utopia the plaque promised to the bathroom as it actually existed, tracked with the footprints of trendy shoes, with a full trash can belching up refuse it couldn't hold, and the corner toilet overflowing, its water quietly seeping under all the stalls. She gave the smug dryer a good slap, smacking it so hard her hand stung.

She shook her hand out and resolved to return to her spot on the balcony. She may have reached the time when she was compelled to become a spectator in her son's life rather than a participant, but she still wanted a good view.

She left the bathroom and headed for the stairs of the balcony. The tattoo woman was still dancing violently, monopolizing the railing. Gwen marched up to her and shoved in beside her. As long as she didn't look the other woman in the eye, her action wouldn't be considered a direct challenge, just some normal crowd jostling, as contact with humanity was inevitable at a concert. Gwen would not budge, no matter how many times the bitch hit her, she was planting her feet shoulder-width apart, keeping her knees slightly bent, gripping the railing with her hands and guarding her territory so that she could look down on Hugh.

Hugh was shouting along with the crowd, pumping his fist in the air when everyone else did. He thrust his elbows out to create more space for himself as everyone surged forward. The woman next to Gwen resumed her pummeling with renewed vigor, and a teenage boy in an immense hooded sweatshirt began to knock Gwen about from the other side. Gwen locked her knees and stood up straight, defending her tiny space. She understood how great rocks must finally submit, after the aggressive erosion of millennia, when they are battered and ready to crumble.

The air was hot and dense, impregnated with the funk of thousands of sweating, excited bodies, the smoke that clung to their clothes and the alcohol on their lips. It seemed to Gwen that everyone in the building was shouting, but the sounds she heard came to her as if from far away, at the end of a long, tinny corridor. Her vision wavered on the edges as she searched again for Hugh. She backed away to an empty corner of the balcony to catch her breath. Her field of sight narrowed to a point, then flicked off.

When Gwen came to, her head was resting in her husband's lap, and Hugh was patting her hand, insisting that she wake up. She looked around, bewildered.

"You passed out," Steven said. "I can't understand why no one around you went for help. There are security guards posted right at the foot of the stairs, not twenty feet away. What kind of people would just let you fall and lie here?"

Gwen had a notion.

"We looked all over for you, Mom," Hugh said. "We had no clue where you were."

Gwen lay on the floor, her head throbbing and her throat parched. The carpeting was soaked in unimaginable substances, yet she had no desire to rise.

"So it's over then, the show," Gwen said.

Hugh nodded.

"Well, did you have a good time?" she asked.

"Considering," Hugh said, his voice hoarse from shouting. But he was smiling, with flushed cheeks and bright eyes. He wore a concert T-shirt he must have bought some time when Gwen wasn't watching, with that weird W in yellow, Wu-Tang written in a font that suggested Mandarin characters.

"They charged ten dollars for a beer, and they wouldn't sell you one without strapping a neon band to your wrist," Steven said. "But we should really get you to a doctor."

"No," she said. "Please, I just need some air." She didn't want to sit in an emergency room. "I just want to get outside and then go home."

When they reached the car, Hugh didn't beg for the front seat as he usually did. He opened the door for his mother, surprising her with a gesture she didn't think was in the vocabulary of kids his age any longer. Her head burbled with unfathomable noises, her hearing so muffled they had to shout to communicate. Gwen glanced back at Hugh and saw him staring out at the sky, his cheek pressed to the cool window, absently tracing with one finger the W on his shirt that covered his chest like a superhero emblem. "Where are we going hiking this weekend?" Hugh asked.

"You still want to go?" Steven asked.

"We always hike on Saturdays," Hugh said. "Let's go somewhere on BLM land so I'm allowed to take rocks for my collection."

Gwen smiled. Hugh was a Wu-Tang-loving teenager, but still an Overby. When they drew near home, they drove up a long hill, and then began the final descent, a portion of the ride that, during the day, gave way to a heart-lifting sight: a pleasant town tucked against extravagant mountains. Gwen couldn't see the mountains in the dark, but she could sense their looming presence. It comforted her to think that there was a mountain so close by, no less a mountain for it being difficult to see. It was there, it was what it was, substantial and unyielding, and nobody could change it.

Signing for Linemen

Kimberly Pritchard shivered in the air-conditioned chill of the athletic building and hesitated by the room where her assigned football players waited. Her research grant hadn't come through, so instead of spending the summer on her *Beowulf* thesis, she would pass it tutoring football players for ten dollars an hour in an athletic building that was as impressive as Heorot, King Hrothgar's grand hall. To prepare, she had spoken to the athletic department's academic advisor about each student and looked them up in the football program's media guide he'd given her, but the advisor's personal notes and the guide's stats on sprint times and weight-lifting records blurred together. She entered the room, finding two football players seated across from each other at a table, slouching in their chairs, their knees spread wide:

> **Javon Green**, 6', 180, Jr. wide receiver out of Pasadena, Calif. Strengths: Runs a 100 in 10.29, was 1-of-1 passing for 25 yards (halfback option) last season, good with the ladies. Weaknesses: Suffered a fractured bone in his right foot last fall, needs to pass 6 hours this summer to be eligible come August.

and

> **Darryl Taggert**, 6'3", 230, Soph. tight end out of Chicago, Ill. Strengths: Earned PrepStar All-America honors in high school, played in

all 11 games (no starts) as a true freshman
last season. Weaknesses: Doesn't like to talk
much around most white people, which hurts
him in participation grades.

Taggert's stomach shuddered audibly and he looked down at it with concern. "Did that check you wrote at the grocery store bounce?" he asked his friend.

"It did *backflips*, dog," Javon said, shaking his head.

Kimberly stood at the door, her glasses pushed up onto her forehead. Why had she decided to wear a blazer, as if she were teaching a class? She should have remembered that she was nothing more than a summer school tutor. As she turned on the light, she imagined her own entry in the media guide:

Kimberly Pritchard, 5'0", 100, 3rd Yr. Ph.D.
student out of Pennington, N.J. Strengths:
Adept at many languages, plays the flute, has
owned a 4.0 GPA since kindergarten, with the
exception of fourth grade when she earned
a C in penmanship. Weaknesses: Socially
awkward, obsessed with medieval literature.

She dropped her book-filled bag on the table with a thud. "I'm Kimberly." She looked from one to the other. "I'll be your language tutor this summer."

The less massive of the two men stood up. "I'm Javon Green," he said with a primetime grin, extending a hand, everything about him golden. He had light brown skin and his dark eyes exuded an intimate warmth. She couldn't hold his gaze.

As she shook his hand, she tried to recall if she'd ever before touched such a physically beautiful man. His lithe strength reminded her of Yul Brynner in *The King and I*, looking like he might perform a handspring at any moment. "Yes," she said absently, "you're on my list."

"This is Darryl Taggert," Javon said, presenting his teammate.

Taggert nodded curtly. He remained seated, his muscled arms crossed over his chest.

"Well, Lil' Kim," Javon said, "I need to pass sign language one and two this summer so I can get that language requirement done."

"I should have taken one more year of Spanish in high school," Taggert said to Javon, ignoring Kimberly. "That class was *easy* at my school. Teacher liked to eat. You just had to bring in Mexican food every Friday."

"But it ain't easy here," Javon said. "I went to Spanish class one day last semester. The teacher wasn't talking *any* English. Shit, I'm taking the class so I can *learn* Spanish. I dropped that for Current Jazz quick."

"Sign language?" Kimberly asked.

"Yeah Miss, that's what we're taking this summer," Javon said.

"I know French, German, Old English, and Italian," she said, laughing nervously. "I do not know sign language."

The smile dropped from Javon's face, his glow dimming. Taggert threw her a look that fairly rumbled.

"I'll go straighten this out." She rushed out the door. She paused two feet down the hallway, realizing she'd forgotten to grab her bag, and turned to fetch it, then reprimanded herself. She was thinking like her boyfriend Chance, who had been printing out articles about various Pac-12 football players' brushes with the law and attaching them to the refrigerator since she accepted the job.

Before her grant was denied, Kimberly had felt sure her proposal for a *Beowulf* website, complete with multimedia presentations in

English and Old English, had outshone the turgid essays submitted by her less technologically adept colleagues. But she'd been the victim of a love triangle in which she wasn't involved and had ended up on the wrong side of the department battle lines. Since she started school, she'd been on a straight path that seemed sure to lead to a Ph.D. and a plum tenure-track position, but suddenly she'd been knocked off course. She hoped the setback in her research wouldn't harm her prospects of landing a good job.

Chance had laughed when she told him about her summer job. "What can you possibly teach those barbarians?" he'd said. "How to scratch themselves with greater efficacy?"

"They're just students, like any others," she'd said. Chance, whose research in the Irish long poem had been funded for the summer, was irritating her now. She was beginning to loathe the way he keened along to Pink Floyd, the way his toes cracked when he walked barefoot, the way he recited Seamus Heaney in an unconvincing brogue. Worse, he remained friendly with Renata, the woman who had won the grant instead. Now Kimberly felt like the Grendel of her department, banished to the fens, seething with grievance.

Kimberly applied to be an athletic department tutor because another grad student told her that the football players never showed for study sessions, so the tutors were paid to sit around and do their own work. The English building lacked air conditioning, and in the summer months it was hard to think through the heat-induced fug in her cubicle, but the athletic building was refreshingly brisk, the floors and ceilings free of mildew and water damage. She had expected to correct a few elementary French compositions during the forty hours she put in a week and consume the rest with her own research. She hoped to make a comeback this summer, perhaps by writing a paper that would be featured at that year's Medieval Studies conference.

"There's been a mistake," Kimberly told the athletic department's academic advisor, a slim man with a neat moustache who always wore khaki slacks and a black or gold sports shirt with the school's logo. In the photo on the wall of him standing in the middle of the football team, he looked like an insect.

"You're good with languages, right?" The advisor barely looked up from his papers.

"I'm proficient in several."

"Then this will be easy. Go to ASL class with them every day, make sure all ten of them show, and check to see they get their assignments done."

"Why sign language?"

"Our guys tend to be visual learners. Plus, the teacher was something of an athlete at one time, so he's sympathetic. You'd be amazed at how many professors see one of our guys walk into their class and write an automatic D in their grade books."

Kimberly nodded, pretending to go along with what she took to be the athletic department's running gripe. She pictured herself leading the football players to class, a hen trailed by her gargantuan chicks. If Renata saw her, she'd probably laugh over it with the other English department powers at one of their brie and Pinot Gris picnics to which Kimberly was never invited. For Kimberly, it had always been about the book itself—her love for *Beowulf.* But for everyone else it seemed to be a cutthroat battle for spoils. She hated how Chance, who handled the English department's mail, never posted fliers for grants and competitions he wanted to enter himself. She'd show them she could work a regular job and still accomplish more than any of them. "All right," Kimberly told the academic advisor. "Where and when is this class held?"

The Professor: Joe Burkhart, 6'0", 200, American Sign Language Ph.D. out of Gallaudet University in Washington, D.C. Strengths: he's deaf and doesn't consider it a weakness, a personable father of two who holds shotput and discus records in the Deaf Olympics. Weaknesses: He can't hear students' cheating whispers during an exam.

The Game: American Sign Language (ASL) 101

Playing Field: RM 210, Knavely Arts and Sciences, no air conditioning.

Game Time: 9 to 11 AM with one 10-minute half time, M-F

The Opponent: TBD

The first morning of ASL class, Kimberly sat in the back and studied the students as they filed into the room. Her football players crowded in: six Black, three white, one Samoan. They sat around the perimeter of the classroom, snug in the high school-style wooden desks, massive legs spread out before them. They wore T-shirts and mesh shorts, their feet in summer sandals. The rest of the students were women in the communications graduate program: five, all white, between the ages of thirty and fifty, several wearing shapeless batik dresses. They sat front and center, glancing back at the football players and whispering among themselves.

Through a hearing interpreter, Joe Burkhart, a barrel-chested man with a silver crew cut, emphasized that he allowed no talking in class. He had a translator for the first day, and after that they would have to overcome their language differences through gestures and signs. It was odd, Kimberly thought, that she couldn't take notes. If she looked down, she had no idea what was going on. Joe demanded constant eye contact. They started with the alphabet, then learned how to introduce themselves and inquire about each other's well-being—standard first semester language stuff. The only sounds as they worked were the wheeze of the ancient air conditioner, noise from the football players shifting in uncomfortable seats, and the faint ticking of the clock.

Kimberly had always enjoyed helping the students that came to her office hours, panicked about writing an essay. She'd take out a clean sheet of paper, convince them to talk about their vague ideas, and jot down anything they said that had an inkling of insight. She'd send the students home with clear plans, their eyes no longer on the verge of tears. But after a few days of ASL class, Kimberly realized that she would be of no use in helping the football players study. She could learn any other language that she'd tried, but she had no memory for ASL. She wrote down the vocabulary words, but what good did that do without a picture? She tried to make crude drawings of Joe's hands, but they flitted from one sign to the next too quickly. There was no textbook. But even with a picture, she couldn't make her hands obey.

The football players understood ASL: no papers to write, no presentations to give. Talk with your hands, that's all, couldn't be simpler. It wasn't much different than learning the play signs the coaches flashed from the sidelines. Not that they would practice ASL unless Kimberly forced them. Sometimes, they told her, Joe lifted weights in the gym when they were there, and they'd sign HELLO to him, inquire HOW YOU?

In class, the grad students sat stiff and straight-faced in their desks, looking sufficiently appalled whenever the guys kidded with

Joe, purposely substituting the sign "SEX" for the sign "MEET," which were similar, the former with two fingers on each hand extended while the fists tapped each other sideways, the latter with one finger extended on each hand while the fists tapped upright. The players couldn't sit comfortably in their desks for long, and when their attention wavered Joe would get the students up and moving, working in groups, signing to each other. He gave them an assignment to write a skit in ASL to perform the following week, the day before the first exam.

A grad student named Cecily, who seemed to be the ringleader, invited Kimberly to join their skit group. Kimberly could guess her stats.

> **Cecily Grassler**, 5'5", 160, 2nd Yr. Ph.D.
> student out of Greeley, CO. Strengths: As
> the sixth child in her family, honed a fierce
> competitive instinct. Won several purple
> ribbons for her dahlia arrangements at the
> Weld county fair. Weaknesses: Unatheltic,
> suffers from chronic cold feet and hands.

Kimberly had no desire to work with the grad students. They reminded her of Renata. "Well, I don't know," she said.

"Lil' Kim's with us," Javon said. "We need a female." He motioned for her to follow him to the corner where two other football players huddled.

Kimberly turned to go, but Cecily caught her arm with her chilly hand and whispered in her ear. "Are you sure? They'll make you do all the work."

"No," Kimberly said. "I can assure you that they won't."

"Suit yourself," Cecily said, turning abruptly to join the other grad students, who were writing down the skit they planned to perform, while the football players joked and signed to each other, working without the medium of English.

Joe circulated to offer help and he bantered easily with the football players, but there was an occasional miscommunication. A tight end wanted to speak about the woman he called his baby mama, compressing the double-arm rocking sign for BABY and the open-handed thumb chin tap for MOTHER together, but no matter how many times he repeated himself, Joe didn't seem to understand.

The grad students signed with rigid formality, hands bobbing from one shape to the next instead of flowing between them. Many of the football players had an inborn grace for ASL, their movements fluid and precise. Even some of the 350-pounders, their eyes squinty from facial bulk, could sign with a casual ease that Kimberly found awe-inspiring, dyslexic with the language as she was.

The skit was due the next day and the first exam approached, but during study hall one afternoon, a lineman refused to focus, drawing the others into a conversation about the respective merits of Hostess and Dolly Madison snack cakes. "Forget Twinkies," said

> **Roland Riddock**, 6'2", 300 Sr. left offensive guard out of Plano, Texas. Strengths: As a high school senior made Dave Campbell's Texas Super Team, allowed only four sacks in 260 pass plays. Weaknesses: Homophobic, addicted to snack cakes.

He pounded his pinkish, freckled fist against the table. "Zingers are the best."

"Yeah," Kimberly said, looking up from her copy of the *C Manuscript*. "Raspberry Zingers."

Riddock gave her a level, serious look, and he did not return her smile. "Just any fuckin' Zinger, man."

Kimberly blinked. "We should go watch the DVD." She could at least sit them in front of the TV and hope they'd absorb something.

"Let's do it tomorrow," Riddock said. "The language lab is too far away."

She needed to be firm, or she'd lose them for the whole study session. "Let's go now." She rose to leave.

The offensive line did not budge. They were sluggish when they weren't working out. They went to fantastic lengths to conserve their energy, stirring only to sign HUNGRY back and forth to each other across the table by making a "C" with the right hand and moving it down the center of the chest from below the throat. They complained to Kimberly that the dining halls were closed and their stipends exhausted. They lived six to a house with no furniture except for mattresses on the ground and the refrigerator that came with the place. They ate cases of ramen noodles and whatever they could beg, bum, sample, or get for free. The coaches gave them money for food and housing, provided that they pass at least three credit hours each summer school session. But the only person who could keep football players sheltered and full on their allowance would be a depression-era farm mother of ten who knew how to turn drippings and scraps from one meal into something miraculously different the next day.

"I don't think I can move," Riddock said. He whined in ASL, signing HUNGRY, HUNGRY, HUNGRY.

"Now," Kimberly ordered. She had some Milk Duds in her backpack. Maybe she'd lure the guys out by dropping a trail.

Eventually they lumbered down the stairs, sweating fluently. They had come straight from their required daily run, all without showering except for:

> **Lamont Strickler**, 6'4", 320, Jr. right offensive guard out of Memphis, Tennessee. Strengths: First-team selection by the Football News last season, led the team in finishing points (similar to pancake blocks) last season, fastidious about grooming. Weaknesses: A mama's boy, not mean enough for the NFL.

They began the walk across campus to the language lab, a journey that usually took Kimberly five minutes, but the guys dragged it out, griping. Javon walked beside her. He was a foot taller than her, and when she turned to the side she saw his golden bicep bulging from his sleeve. She thought of a line about Beowulf: *There was no one else like him alive.* "So what's your story, Lil' Kim?" he asked. "How come you're tutoring us this summer?"

"Didn't get my grant," she said.

"Why not?" He looked at her directly, seeming genuinely interested.

After weeks of complaining about the incident to Chance, he'd forbidden her to bring it up. "It's like this," she began. "One of the deans of the College of Arts and Sciences was dating a much-younger English professor who was promoted to the department chair. Everyone thought she'd slept her way into her position, so when the dean dumped her, she wanted to assume more responsibility to prove her worth. So she took over the research grant proposal committee. She also began dating Renata, another Ph.D. student in my department, and gave her the grant I applied for, even though Renata had just switched topics a few weeks earlier and had barely done any research." She pictured Renata's snotty moue, her sharp little nose dotted with a ruby on the left side, the glint of her dyed black cherry hair. Kimberly clenched her fists, but stopped herself from saying more, feeling suddenly abashed.

Javon didn't speak for a moment as they walked along the concrete path. "Damn," he said, finally.

"I'm sorry," Kimberly said. She never spoke like this to her students. There was something about the heat of summer and the deserted campus that had relaxed her into forgetting what she'd learned her first semester teaching: if you get too personal with your students, they'll get too personal with you. "I shouldn't have told you," she said.

"Sure you should've. I just wondered why you were stuck with us is all." He put his hand on her shoulder. Her heart trilled. "Just keep doing what you're doing," he said. "Those fools will soon realize they can't mess with Lil' Kim."

Javon's nickname for her had spread to all the football players. She hadn't told Chance about it, because he'd only mock it. She imagined breaking up with him and buying herself a pair of spike heels, getting a tattoo of a tiger's paw raking her left breast like the one sported by a rap star on the cover of a magazine Taggert brought to study hall. She'd stuck to one plan for her whole life, but now fantasized about other possible selves.

When they reached the language lab, Kimberly passed her student I.D. to the clerk for collateral and took the DVD into one of the cramped viewing rooms. The players settled in as best they could, three sizes too large for furniture built for regular humans. When any of them belched, farted, or made a remark about female anatomy, they glanced at her, a sheepish check for her reaction. She imagined it had been like this for the women in King Hrothgar's mead hall.

The DVD series featured the Bravo family, a jovial crew, who did things like visit the grocery store together. The mother woke her children for breakfast by kissing them on their cheeks. The narrator, Billy Seago, who always wore a black turtleneck, could stop the family's action at any time and appear in the middle of the living room to explain the vocabulary while the Bravo family remained frozen. As the DVD explained, in ASL a signer must raise his eyebrows when asking yes or no questions. When asking who, what, when, where, why, or how, the signer must furrow his brow.

The Bravo family was having a good time at the grocery store. They didn't smile—they beamed. They didn't laugh—they silently guffawed. Their exaggerated facial expressions resembled bad acting.

"Why do they have to be so *dramatic* about everything?" Javon asked. "Are there any Black deaf folks?"

"I wonder if they have deaf porno," Riddock said.

"I hate this!" Strickler threw down his notebook. "They do the signs all differently than Joe does. How am I supposed to know which way to do them?"

"Joe's always right," Riddock said. "I like Joe. These other guys are idiots." He pounded his notebook with his fist. "*Billy Seago*," he said, with contempt.

"Don't you think you should be paying attention to the video?" Kimberly asked.

"Aw, we know this stuff," Riddock said. "This is just review." He pressed the fast forward button and scanned through it. "See, they're only just now teaching numbers. We learned numbers on the first day."

Kimberly tried to remember the numbers, whispering to herself by keeping her hands low, extending her index finger twice, rapidly, for eleven. Javon saw her.

"Look," he said, "one, two, three, four," counting with his hands so that she could see. She counted along with him. "Do you have to pass this class too?"

"NO," she signed, bringing her right thumb, index and middle fingers together a few times.

"That sucks," he said. "You should at least get some credits for the class."

"I don't need any credits." She'd started college as an undergraduate with enough AP credits to skip two semesters, and finished two degrees in the time it took most to complete a B.A. She felt as though she'd been born with credits, and the credits had a weight to them she could no longer bear. Sometimes she wanted to abandon her studies and go forth into the world, swinging her hips, the way women with no credits did.

Yet, Beowulf awaited her like a neglected lover. She wondered how many of Grendel's problems were caused by the fact that he couldn't speak. As she had explained on her website, Anglo-Saxon society prized verbal prowess, and so speechless Grendel was remembered only as a villain in other people's poems and not as the hero of his own. She knew she should be working on her thesis, but she had developed an obsession with ASL, reviewing signs at night with a visual dictionary on the Internet. Chance occasionally looked at her screen over her shoulder and called it a waste of time. She could now produce many of the individual signs, but her sentences didn't flow the way the guys' did.

Kimberly dressed carefully the next morning for the skit performance, trying to figure out how to portray her role: an attractive woman at a bar. She was nervous about performing with Javon, Riddock, and Strickler. She settled on a black halter dress with an A-line skirt and a cherry pattern that she'd bought on a whim and hadn't yet been bold enough to wear. *Why the hell not?* she decided. When Chance saw her before she left, he trailed his fingertips along her waist and asked, "Why would you wear that dress?"

She'd shrugged. "It's summer. I'm wearing a summer dress."

But when she walked into class, she saw everyone else had worn regular clothes. She cursed her knack for always wearing the inappropriate thing. When it was time to begin, she reluctantly stood and joined her group.

"You look beautiful," Strickler said in his charming Memphis lilt.

Javon spun her. "Lil' Kim," he said, "stepping out." He rapped Riddock on his fleshy pink arm. "Don't she look good?"

Riddock swallowed a mouthful of glazed doughnut he'd boasted about snatching from a freshman orientation spread on the way to class. "Like a cherry Zinger."

Javon clutched his heart with both hands and looked at her as he faded back. Kimberly knew this was a cheesy gesture, and that there was no scenario in which she and Javon would ever be together. But being near him awakened some hunger in her.

The communications grad students performed their skit first, a scene about a mishap in buying fruit at the grocery store that was tame and cheery enough to have been lifted from the Bravo family videos. Kimberly's group went next. She sat on a chair that was meant to be a barstool, and ordered a glass of wine from Strickler, circling a W hand around her mouth. Riddock walked into the bar, did an exaggerated double take in Kimberly's direction, then signed, "HEY BABY, WHAT'S YOUR SIGN?" Kimberly turned her back to him and crossed her arms over her chest. Then Javon entered the bar and hit on Riddock, using the same pick-up line, which the guys had been proud of memorizing. Riddock signed, "I'M NOT GAY," and the two got into a dispute, throwing in every coarse and dirty sign they knew. Meanwhile, Kimberly and Strickler the bartender flirted, batting their eyelashes at each other, and at the end of the skit, Kimberly and Strickler linked arms and walked off, and Riddock and Javon linked arms and left in the opposite direction.

The grad students asked Joe to explain some of Riddock's colorful vocabulary. As Joe fingerspelled and wrote on the chalkboard to translate, Cecily shook her head. Earning Cecily's disapproval felt like a win for Kimberly's team.

Joe continued the vocabulary lesson, but one of the younger women spoke aloud when his back was turned to the chalkboard. "That's hardly appropriate."

"They shouldn't be using that kind of language in the classroom," Cecily said.

"ASL is just like any other language," Kimberly said. "If you learn only words that are pretty or kind, you don't know the half of it."

Cecily turned around and shushed her with an exaggerated motion so Joe noticed and signed "NO TALK" to Kimberly.

She signed "SORRY," rubbing her heart with her fist, and then stared at the back of Cecily's head, picturing it hanging from Heorot's rafters. The women considered themselves sensitive to the deaf community. They laughed too loud and long at Joe's most frivolous jokes and made a show of their outrage when Joe told the story about a deaf man who'd been pulled over by the cops and was shot as he reached for a pad and pen to communicate with the officer. But they couldn't make Joe love them best, so they invented a new competition—the women began sending an early emissary to the language lab after class so they could beat the football players to the lone copy of the DVD.

Joe called for a ten-minute break after the skits, and Kimberly spent it checking off the boxes next to the football players' names on her attendance sheet and asking the guys for their grades on the last quiz. When Kimberly went to get a drink of water in the hallway, Cecily and the grad students followed.

"What were you doing, taking attendance?" Cecily asked, smiling aggressively.

"I have to make sure the football players come to class," Kimberly explained. "It's my job."

"That's ridiculous," Cecily said. The other four murmured in agreement. "Who pays your salary?"

"The athletic department."

"So taxpayers' money goes toward baby-sitting football players." Cecily's pack was nodding, *Sing it sister*.

"Just a minute," Kimberly said, heat rising in her face. "The football players bring in more revenue than any other part of this university. And what do they get?"

Cecily's jaw twitched. Kimberly knew she had crossed over in Cecily's perception, from one of us to one of them. And Lil' Kim liked that.

That day at study hall, the football players sat around, looking at sports magazines, begging barbecue chips from the center who was foolish enough to stuff a bag of them in his backpack, forgetting the telltale crinkle would give his stash away.

"Guys, come on, the test's tomorrow," Kimberly prodded.

"Don't worry, Lil' Kim," Strickler said, settling his ball cap over his eyes and leaning back in the chair for a nap, "we know the stuff."

"Hey," Riddock said, "you're in the English department, right?"

"Yes," Kimberly said, eager to redeem herself as a tutor. "I could help you with an essay."

"No, I just wanted to know something." He leaned forward, his massive fingers interlaced on the table before him. "Javon says the English Department is full of Peppermint Patties."

Kimberly flinched. Javon had told everyone about her problems. Used it as fodder for jokes. She looked at Javon, who sat at the computer in the corner of the room. What had she been thinking, that the golden boy of the football team was her friend? He probably couldn't help but deploy his charms on any female he encountered.

"I've got to get some English credits in the fall," Riddock continued. "Could you tell me which professors to avoid?" He signed LESBIAN, resting an L-shaped hand against his cheek and chin. "Peppermint Patties hate football players."

"I'm sure that's not true," Kimberly said. Riddock had probably taken care to choose the least offensive synonym for lesbian that he could think of. She considered lecturing him about tolerance and appropriate terminology, but decided the lesson wouldn't sink in.

"The other English teachers are probably hassling you because they want you," Riddock counseled. "Sexually."

Kimberly wished it were as simple as that. Then she'd just have to walk around the English department dressed like Lil' Kim on the cover of "La Bella Mafia"—suspenders with no shirt, a look on her face that dared anyone to question her fashion choice—to win the grants she needed.

In class the morning of the exam, Joe Burkhart made conversation, trying to loosen them up, asking people how they had spent the weekend before.

"WEEKEND LAST," Javon signed, "I GO TO BAR. SEE BAD LOOKING WOMEN."

The football players busted up. The women frowned and met each other's disapproving glances. Kimberly had spent Saturday with Chance, watching three Luis Buñuel movies in a row, as she'd promised. Chance had played the scene of the eyeball being stabbed in *Un Chien Andalou* over and over. She wished she could have gone out with the football players instead, to the bar where people threw the shells of free peanuts on the floor.

Kimberly took the exam so that she could measure her progress. As Joe signed sentences for them to translate, traced shapes in the air for them to draw, and signed a floor plan of an imaginary building for them to write down, she became utterly lost. If she were getting graded she would have flunked. She let out a burst of laughter under her breath at the thought. It felt like being in one of those test taking nightmares that other people had—Kimberly had never had one, as school used to be her ace. Riddock, two desks over from her, enjoined himself to succeed. "Come on," he whispered to himself, "I know this."

The next day, the academic advisor told Kimberly that four of the football players had been accused of cheating on the exam.

"That is bull shit," Javon insisted when he learned he was one of the accused. He signed the expletive for emphasis, placing his right arm on top of the left arm, elbow to hand, making bull horns by extending the curled index and pinky finger of his right hand, and waving the fingers of the left hand rapidly underneath. "It was them stupid old ladies who did it."

The academic advisor brought the accused into his office one at a time. He seemed experienced in such matters. He spoke to Kimberly first. "Those women don't even know the football player's names," she told him. "How could they know whom to accuse?"

"Did you see or hear anything?" he asked.

"Riddock was talking to himself under his breath a little. Some of them were signing to themselves so they knew how to answer the questions. But they kept their hands under their desks. Nobody did anything improper." She fumed at the thought of Cecily, who would have fit right in at Renata's gatherings.

The women had fingered Javon, Taggert, Riddock, and Strickler. Kimberly imagined them huddled around the football media guide, flipping through the scouting reports until they recognized a picture. After the individual conversations, the academic advisor told the ten football players and Kimberly to assemble in the conference room for a meeting. Kimberly sat pinned in the far corner of the room packed with male flesh, worrying that she'd let them down, that she'd be kicked off the team.

"Hey, Tag," Javon shouted across the table to Taggert, "So I go over to study at some girl's house, and I see your clothes there."

The guys looked up, with interest.

"*What?*" Taggert asked.

"You saying that wasn't your hat?"

"Oh, you see," Taggert said, turning to the cornerback next to him. "Now he's saying my hat. First he said my clothes."

"I'm just saying, your *apparel*. You never see *my* apparel at some girl's house."

"That's because you take them back to *your* house."

The guys laughed. As the parade of Javon's beautiful women ran through Kimberly's imagination, she felt a pang, then rebuked herself for it. She thought of her pop-up window about boasting in *Beowulf*, which informed the website user that in Anglo-Saxon society, boasts were, in essence, vows.

While the laughter faded, Riddock turned to Lamont Strickler, contemplating him, the only quiet one in the bunch. "I saw your mom the other day when she visited," Riddock said. Strickler nodded. Javon had told Kimberly that Strickler was occasionally overwhelmed by a bout of homesickness, and his mother would come up from Memphis and cook everyone a vat of ribs drenched in her homemade barbecue sauce.

"She doesn't look like you," Riddock said. "Are you mixed?"

"Fool, look at him," Taggert said. "Mixed with what? His mom's Black and his dad's Black as hell?"

The whole room started hooting and the table quivered from the guys' powerful belly laughs.

"Quiet!" Kimberly shouted, standing up suddenly.

The room silenced and they looked over to her.

"These are serious allegations," she said. "Don't you know that?"

"Lil' Kim's right," Javon said, "We could get kicked out of summer school, plus we got to pay back the stipend and tuition."

Everyone started to complain and hiss. The academic advisor entered the room, and they all began shouting at once.

Riddock shook his head. "I need this language class to graduate. I'm not going back to Texas with 130 credits and no diploma."

"Man," Strickler said, "There's no way I could pay that stipend back."

"Who else has been accused?" Javon wanted to know.

"Just us four," Taggert said, "and we weren't even sitting near each other."

"I'm taking one for the race," Riddock insisted. "Those ladies knew they couldn't just accuse three Black guys of cheating. So they threw me in."

"Hold it now," the advisor said, raising his hands. "Nothing has been proven. I'm going to meet with your teacher and the director of the ASL program this afternoon. For now, Coach Brutlag wants to talk to you."

Brutlag, the linebacker coach, was the only member of the team's staff who was not then vacationing in a tropical isle. He had a massive head and a sun-blasted face.

"Listen up, men," he said. "This is going to be quick."

The guys sat up in their chairs and drew their knees closer together.

"As members of the football team, you are representatives of this university. The outcome of this case hasn't been decided, so from now on, I want you to behave so that you are above reproach. You got that?"

They nodded in unison. Brutlag rested his black Nike on a chair, and leaned his elbow on his leg, his polyester coaching shorts stretching taut against his bulk.

"No talking in class at all," he continued. "These old bags are riding your asses. Don't give them any excuse to accuse you." He stared at them with an intensity in his ice blue eyes that frightened Kimberly. "Be above reproach," he repeated. "Now I've got to make my tee time. I don't want to be called in here again."

He left. The room remained silent for a moment.

"Tomorrow," Javon said, "Let's go to class early and take the front seats from those ladies."

The guys grinned.

"I could take that test again," Riddock said, "and nail it, just like last time." He pounded his fist on the table. Everyone began to shout, rallying for battle against the five women with spider-veined legs. Kimberly now knew what it felt like to want to ram into a tackling dummy, grunting and growling, or to gird a sword on her thigh and rush out to claim the head of a foe.

That afternoon when Kimberly was about to leave work, the academic advisor called her into his office. He told her that he'd met with the teacher and the director of the Sign Language department. "The director trusts those grad students," he said. "He didn't think they would falsely accuse anybody of cheating."

Yeah, Kimberly thought, *grad students are always so honest and forthright.* "The guys didn't cheat," she said. She waited for him to fire her, digging her fingernails into the moist flesh of her palms.

"Well, there's no way to prove the allegations," he continued. "Joe insisted on this point. So the guys are getting off with a warning. You're going to have to keep them in line for the rest of the session, though, because they won't get a second chance." He looked at her sternly, issuing an unspoken reprimand.

"You're still under scrutiny," Kimberly told the football players the next day before they headed from the athletic building to the classroom. "No talking in class, period. And from now on, Joe is going to have a hearing assistant sit in class and listen to you during the test." She thought of Beowulf's words, *Fate often saves an undoomed man when his courage is good.*

The football players moved faster than Kimberly had ever seen them as they hustled over to the class building. They arrived ten minutes early and sat in a phalanx, filling the front two rows. When the women arrived, they stared at the guys, as if willing them to move, and then picked their way to the back, having difficulty finding a path past the big men.

"I can't see back here," Kimberly heard Cecily stage whisper, "They're just huge."

Cecily went up to the front of the room before class started and scribbled a note to Joe on a piece of paper. He looked at it and then stood, gesturing for the hearing monitor to address the class. "Professor Burkhart wanted me to come in and explain this in

English so there are no misunderstandings," the monitor said. "I'll be sitting in during tests from now on. And there is to be no talking, period, or it will cost you your grade." NO TALK, Joe signed.

Joe opened the door for the monitor to leave, taking back control of the classroom, his eyes fierce. Kimberly wondered if he was angry that the accusations had forced him to use an assistant during tests, as though he couldn't run the class himself.

Joe abruptly turned to the board and wrote "COMPETITION," across the top, the chalk squeaking as he finished the word. He turned to them and signed the instructions. They were to split into three teams and form lines. When he gave the signal, the first person in each line would draw a notecard with a word on it, which they would have to sign to the next teammate in line, who would write the word on the chalkboard.

The women immediately formed a line, and Joe smirked at them, as if to let them know that he expected no less. The football players sorted themselves into two groups, the four accused cheaters sticking together. Kimberly sat at her desk, scribbling some notes about the new ideas for research she'd had after the first fallow weeks of summer, on the bonds of kinship among warrior athletes. But Javon drew her into the back of his line. She looked at him and he smiled. "WE NEED YOU," he signed, the last word ending with his index finger pointed at her. Joe raised his hands, then dropped them, and the first person in each line raced to the stack of cards while the second person rushed to the board.

The smell of chalk dust filled the air and the game moved almost too quickly for Kimberly to keep up with it. Strickler drew a card and performed the sign for "STRONG," and Riddock scrawled the word on the board. They drew "YELLOW" and "TOY" and "GUEST." Kimberly was terrified that she'd get words she didn't know how to sign, but she got lucky, drawing "BALL" and "HOUSE" and "WOMAN." Joe walked among the students, correcting the positioning of their hands. The guys were pumped, racing up to the desk for the card and pounding back to the end of the line so that the floor of the room shook, and on one turn Riddock clipped a desk, sending it crashing to the ground.

Kimberly glanced at the grad students' progress. Cecily tried to draw a card, but couldn't pick it up, and had to lick her finger to grip the paper. She signed "CAT," and the woman at the board wrote "TIGER." Cecily shook her head and signed again, stroking whiskers with her fingertips, while the woman at the board shrugged and shook her head. The room was silent except for the sound of the football players' pounding feet and the occasional squeak of chalk across the board.

Joe flicked the lights on and off to signal the end of the game. The two teams of football players had lists of words twice as long as those of the grad students. Joe checked the words on the board against the cards, crossed off a few wrong answers, then took up Javon's hand and the hand of a center. Joe paused, then threw Javon's arm in the air.

The accused cheaters went nuts, in silence, jumping and slapping each other's hands, bumping chests, celebrating the way they were not allowed to in the end zone. Kimberly applauded in ASL, raising her arms and fluttering her hands like windblown boughs, and Riddock lifted her into the air, her skirt flaring as she rose. A squeal escaped her, a sound she hadn't made since she was playing four square on the elementary school blacktop. She covered her mouth with her hand, and as she looked down over the classroom, she imagined the revelry that followed Beowulf's triumphant return with the head of the beast on a spear.

"Oh for heaven's sake," Cecily said. "It's just a game."

Joe pointed at her. "NO TALK," he signed, then picked up his grade book to mark down her infraction. She threw up her hands.

Joe flicked the lights on and off to calm them down. Everyone settled into their desks, but Kimberly could feel the exuberance from the victory still coursing off the players, Javon nudging Taggert and miming swishing a basketball through a hoop. As Joe signed, Kimberly could picture them all assembled in bright Heorot, its rafters rising above, good King Hrothgar thanking Beowulf after the defeat of two monsters for fostering friendship and peace between peoples, the King's Danes and Beowulf's Geats. And the young warriors lining the mead-hall benches, rapt, clad in beaten-gold mail, their glinting helmets and swords at rest as they vowed to serve each other unto death, the courage-giving weight of warrior's armor on their shoulders.

Community Relations

The letters came to Ada opened, and spoke of rare disease. They were typed, respectful, addressed to one of the three ballplayers with the highest batting averages or to the pitcher with the wickedest curve, and their authors always mentioned in the opening line that they were writing on behalf of a young relative who was suffering from a rare disease. Why did everyone choose the word "rare"? Why not "nasty" or "dread" or even "God-damned"? If someone would cuss in a cancer letter, she would send him a prize. But they weren't interested in her, of course, and when they wrote their earnest letters they probably never imagined that someone like Ada would read them.

The letters poured in during the height of the season and a secretary skimmed them to determine whether they were simply teeming with chatty homage or if they had a more urgent purpose. The fan mail from children went to the Rockies Rookies Club manager, who would respond with a flimsy reproduction of a marginally recent black-and-white team photo and an application to join the kids' club. The letters from vengeful kooks went to the head of stadium security. The sick mail came to Ada, who was the lowest-ranking employee in the Community Relations department of the Colorado Rockies Baseball Club.

You could practically chart how well a guy was playing by the volume of sick mail he received. Some of them got stacks of it, but still all the letters contained that word "rare." Ada couldn't decide how it was intended. Was the only acceptable way for the relatives to express their sublimated anger to point out how unlikely it was that this disease would strike anyone? Or was it meant as a comfort: don't fear, it's not an epidemic, it's not contagious, none of the baseball players will catch anything if you do us this one kindness. There were so many letters Ada wondered how they managed it in ball clubs that actually won pennants. The Yankees must have served as the locus of desperation for hundreds of sick children. Ada hated the Yankees, a team with money, championships, and history the Rockies could only dream of.

Ada's boss, Chip, popped his head into her cubicle. "Who's set for the Care and Share tonight?" He liked to know what was going on, though he couldn't handle meeting the sick kids. He had a new baby and the illnesses of children spooked him. His first week back from paternity leave, he'd accompanied Ada on a Care and Share, and a frail, ginger-haired little girl got sick while watching batting practice, puking on Chip's loafers. He'd gritted out a smile and told her it was all right, but then vanished to clean his shoes and never returned. Instead he focused on the team's program of building little league fields around the state. He approved the plans, visited the sites, and selected the type of dirt, always trying to convince the players to donate more money so they could add Soilmaster Red Stabilizer to the Brown Premium Diamond Tex Infield Mix on these fields.

"It was supposed to be a kid named Milo, but his dad just called and said they had to cancel again," Ada said, looking at the calendar where she penciled in the names of guests. "He's sick from chemo."

"Three reschedules? That's pushing it."

This isn't a hair appointment, she wanted to say. "We've already picked another date." They hadn't set another date, actually. Ada told Milo's dad that if he ever was feeling well on a game day, he should just call before they left and then come. She would work out the details.

Chip took the calendar out of Ada's hands. "There are plenty of kids who want to do this that will actually show up." On the whiteboard in his office Chip tallied all the Little League fields they'd built, all the kids they'd run through a Care and Share, all the items and tickets they'd donated to charity.

Ada smiled and nodded. "What can you do?"

There were tickets to distribute to nonprofits and a letter to write from the centerfielder to a bedridden boy, but then Sherrie walked in. Sherrie was in Operations and they went to lunch together. Ada wasn't sure how it happened. It seemed as though Sherrie had appropriated her somehow, just after Ada had been promoted from Ticketing and moved up to the second floor. Sherrie had stopped by the first day to say hello and had immediately launched into a discussion of the private details of her life, revealing untoward matters of lust, finance, and gynecology. Sherrie startled Ada with the way she spoke like the women did on bawdy morning radio shows, but when Sherrie asked her to go to lunch, Ada agreed.

They went across the street to one of the fashionable restaurants in red brick warehouses that had sprung up when Coors Field opened, trying to look historic and chic at the same time. Sherrie had thick, dark hair halfway down her back, steeled buns and mastered thighs. Ada felt like an anthropologist when she watched the way men looked at Sherrie. Dinger, the Rockies' purple triceratops mascot, was the only man who ever looked at Ada that way. Men in business attire checked Sherrie out over ducked menus, and outside, the construction workers hollered at her like coyotes at a blue moon. But Sherrie was focused on working her way through the entire team, married or not. Of course she wouldn't succeed, because some of the ballplayers didn't do that sort of thing, they had been saved by Jesus or loved their wives, or suspected that Jesus loved their wives, or would be traded or sent down to the minors before their turn in Sherrie's rotation came up, but still, Sherrie always had a development to report.

Ada didn't think it was jealousy that drew her to Sherrie, more of a clinical fascination. Ada knew she'd never be a red-lipped woman a man would want to steal away and tango with. Not someone you'd write a song about. Ada was a blonde with bangs that curled meekly under and steadfast brown eyes, not like Sherrie's melting chocolate, light-catching, thick-eyelashed ones. Ada wore pressed khakis almost every day and was built like a boy. She was incapable of flirting, simply didn't know how it was done. She was twenty-five and had never had a boyfriend. She wondered what would it be like to have a summer fling. To feel young enough to sneak out of the house at night. But she had always felt old, or as though an old person had taken up permanent residence on her chest, making her think better of getting up and going out.

There was nothing wrong with Ada that anyone could see. But Ada saw it every day. When she undressed for the night, her eyes were drawn to the faint blue dots tattooed on her skin when she was younger so that the radiation treatments could be positioned exactly each time. Ada tried not to think about what future calamities the radiation might cause—skin cancers, new tumors, unavoidable weight gain. She'd stopped reading the results of studies that showed survivors of childhood cancer were less likely to graduate from college and get married than their healthy siblings. She tried not to spend too much time wishing they'd developed today's leukemia therapies back when she was sick, so she'd have gotten off radiation-free. Ada supposed she continued to tolerate Sherrie because she hardly asked Ada any questions. Sherrie had too much to tell, and the last thing Ada wanted to talk about was herself.

"Guess which player," Sherrie said, beaming, as they sat down to lunch.

"I have no idea," Ada said. "I couldn't guess." Ada rooted for some of the players to hold out so that she could maintain her respect for them. Resisting Sherrie couldn't have been much harder than hitting a knuckleball. But many of them capitulated.

"The centerfielder." Sherrie sank back in her chair, satisfied.

"No," Ada said. "He's married. Please tell me that you made that up. He was good."

"Damn right he's good!" Sherrie said with unrepentant glee.

Ada sighed. She felt like every utterance she made around Sherrie was the set-up for some sort of sexual pun. At times she wished she could click her heels together and whisk Sherrie back into a Jackie Collins novel where she belonged. As Sherrie divulged the specifics, Ada chose a spot on her flawless forehead to stare at and tried not to listen. The centerfielder was Ada's favorite because he sprinted to his position every inning, ran out even pitiful grounders and always signed the children's baseballs. Last home stand she brought a little boy with heart troubles down on the field to watch batting practice and the centerfielder took one look at him and said, "Don't go anywhere until I have a chance to sign his ball. I have to go get taped, but stay right there." The boy was gaunt, all eyes and bone. The color of his dark brown skin was off, as though covered with a layer of gray ash. He wore a white T-shirt and his mother held an umbrella over him to shield him from the sun. His face was so solemn he seemed wise, and he accepted each autograph with Lincoln-like gravity.

The centerfielder returned and whispered to Ada, "What's the matter with him?"

"It's his ticker," Ada said.

The centerfielder ran down to the dugout and grabbed one of his bats from the wooden cubby, took the boy's pen and signed it. Then he shed his warm-up jacket, signed the kid's ball and handed it all to him. The centerfielder wasn't satisfied yet, so he peeled off his left batting glove and added that to the pile. The boy smiled as he struggled to hold it all. His mother said softly, "God bless you." Ada was pleased. This guy actually cared.

But how was she going to write a letter from him to a sick kid now? She usually tried to match what she thought the voice of each player would be. She made the tobacco-spitting catcher—who seemed the sort of fellow prone to excessive use of exclamation points—say things like: "You're going to clobber your disease! You'll be socking them to the fence in no time!" In the letters from the Christian shortstop with the golden cross on a chain around his neck, Ada would throw in some Jesusy talk. When she wrote as several members of the pitching staff, Ada added Spanish phrases for authenticity, *qué lástima, qué mala suerte*, because none of them spoke any English at all.

After lunch, when Ada started writing the letter from the centerfielder, she entered default mode, focusing on the child she was writing to, not the Sherrie-succumbing ballplayer the message was supposed to be from. "I'm always sorry to hear that a fan of mine is ill," Ada typed. "Your courage is an inspiration to me." She fell into the language people used when talking about unlucky children, the Wednesday's Child dictionary of sappy uplift and hope. There was an entire canon of treacle to direct at the families of sick kids. *She's a fighter. He's a soldier.* Ada had heard it all before and hated it, but she couldn't say anything better because there wasn't anything better to say.

Would she have bought this banal tripe when she was a sick little kid, if it had come on a sheet of Kansas City Royals letterhead with George Brett's unassailable signature at the bottom? This letter would be framed, Ada felt certain, it would be framed and hung on the wall next to this boy's bed or placed on his nightstand and if he didn't make it, after he was gone it would remain in the room just as it was for years, becoming a part of the family's shrine to their child's memory. She was a horrible person to introduce this fake letter into that scene. But what was worse, if the kid got no reply, or if he received a letter that wasn't actually written by his hero, but didn't know the difference?

When it was over, they'd called her the miracle kid. For years afterward Ada had felt close enough to God to sense his breath. She thought about how in the Bible they never say what happened to Lazarus after he was raised. He'd been dead. How did he live with that knowledge? What happened to the blind that Jesus gave sight? Did they understand what they saw, or did they always have to feel something to know it?

She finished the letter and brought it to Chip, who would then take it down to the locker room and have the centerfielder sign it. He read it and nodded his approval. "Is this kid too sick to do a Care and Share?"

"He's bedridden."

"Then we'll send Dinger over to visit."

"I don't know," Ada said. The last thing she would have wanted to see while she was in the hospital was a big purple dinosaur with stoned plastic eyes, a trippy polka-dotted head frill, and a maniacal grin.

"Kids love Dinger," her boss said, giving her a stern look.

Ada wondered how Chip would talk about these children if he knew about her past. She made sure no one found out. A friend she'd made in the hospital had warned her about job interviewers. Some had discovered his history and then didn't hire him, without explaining why. Ada was careful to send her resume only to businesses with large workforces so her health insurance application would go through. She remembered everyone's advice when she went for the interview with the Rockies: steer the conversation away from your past so that you don't have to lie about what happened to you, about why you were so old when you finished high school, why you had to earn a G.E.D. It hadn't come up and Ada got the job and her parents took her out for a steak dinner, where they drank too much wine and held hands across the table in their happiness over this slight relief from the burden that Ada was to them.

"You're right," Ada said, plastering on a smile. "Kids love Dinger."

"Absolutely. Oh, and I managed to set up a last-minute Care and Share for tonight to replace the cancellation."

Last minute? Ada wondered what this was. Sick kids and their families weren't big whimmers. Their lives were ruled by chemo's aftermath, doctor appointments, the need for sleep. *Hey, I have an idea! Let's go to the ballpark!* was not something they said. Ada's boss handed her a slip of paper with a name on it. "Corey Pearlmutter?" she said. "He's been here before. Twice."

"He's thirteen years old and in a wheelchair!" Ada's boss said, shaking his head. "You'll meet him an hour and a half before first pitch."

"Of course." Corey Pearlmutter was the only kid who had ever annoyed Ada. A disease had left him paralyzed from the waist down but otherwise healthy and preternaturally chipper, plucky, golden-haired, cherubic. Just what everyone seemed to want in a sick kid. He was too casual from the start, didn't evince enough awe as she led him through the secret tunnels under the stadium. "Here," she pointed out with what she thought was sufficient bravado, "the private quarters of the umpires." But that didn't impress him at all. Not even the players' daycare facilities or weight room elicited a reaction.

"Do I get to eat dinner with Dante Bichette? Or Andres Galaraga? Or both of them? I ate dinner with John Elway," he said, interrupting her talk about the players' conditioning workouts. Corey Pearlmutter had dined with Elway and Patrick Roy, served as poster child for three different organizations, and had helped carry the Olympic torch twice. The road to public office seemed to pass through Corey Pearlmutter's house—all major Colorado statesmen in Corey's lifetime posed for a picture with him before being elected. She wanted to tell him: *You'll come out onto the field and stay in the designated area and keep your mouth closed while I ask the players to sign your ball but only the bullpen catcher and the pitching coach will approach and you'll love it kid, you'll shut up and love it.*

So Ada hauled the Care and Share sign down to the front of the stadium and waited with a smile on her face for the arrival of Corey Pearlmutter. Last time Corey had brought an entourage. They'd set aside six tickets for him and he'd shown up with twice that many people, and when Ada had told them that it was impossible, the Rockies were playing the Cubs and the game sold out months earlier, Ada's boss had rushed down and found all the seats they needed, upgraded to club level. Somehow the whole thing was made out to be Ada's fault. So Ada stood, grinning, next to the Care and Share sign. Care and Share. She hated the name of the program. She would have called it something else. Dinger's Kids. The Wrecked Body Autograph Club. Pals of The Reaper.

"Hello Corey," Ada said, smiling so much her face hurt. Even if she didn't have a boyfriend, at least she had a nemesis. He'd brought at least two-dozen people with him, but it didn't matter, the Expos were here and he could have had the whole west stands if he needed them, they could all link hands and sway to "Oh Canada" together.

"Ada!" Corey shouted. "How've you been?"

Who was this kid? Care and Shares didn't call her by her first name. They didn't call her anything at all. "Peachy," Ada said.

"I've brought some friends."

"So I see."

"I didn't know if I wanted to come, seeing how the Expos are here today, but it's a great evening for a ballgame. I was supposed to sign autographs at the Bonfils blood drive, but I decided to blow them off."

"Well, I'm happy you could join us then." Usually the parents did all the talking, but Corey was clearly the leader of his sizable band. She led Corey's posse through the lobby to the elevators down to the stadium tunnels. She had to ride up and down three times to transport them all, swiping her I.D. each time. When Ada finished bringing the last group down, Corey was regaling his people with a tale, something about the time he'd met Streisand at a benefit concert, and they were laughing. "Oh, Ada," he said, "I meant to give you this."

She took a piece of paper from his hand. "What is this?"

"It's a list of players whose autographs I need. I've brought their rookie cards with me to get them signed."

"Gee Corey, I don't have any control over which players choose to sign autographs on any given day. You see, they're at work here, and some of them really need to concentrate on getting ready for the game."

"Yes, you've told me that before. I'm sure you'll do all you can." Corey held out his hand to her.

Ada looked down. He'd slipped her a twenty. She tried to give it back to him, but he'd already rolled his wheelchair away toward the field. They emerged behind home plate and Ada sent the rest of Corey's troops to sit in the nearby seats. She wheeled Corey out toward the dugout, avoiding the freshly chalked on-deck circle. She faced Corey. "You know the drill by now. We wait here and watch batting practice, and as they come back to the dugout I see if I can snag them to sign your ball."

"And my rookie cards."

It was not the best autograph day. Many of the players were friendly with members of the Expos and they hung around behind the metal batting practice cage, spitting and slapping each other on the back. The pitchers were almost never around at this point, so at first Ada could only find back-up infielders to sign Corey's ball. She was wearing a sleeveless blouse and the second-string shortstop brushed her bare shoulder with his calloused hand, saying *Excuse me, honey,* as he made his way to the dugout. Ada's heart fluttered. But then Dinger waddled over, stole Ada's hairclip and attached it to her nose, the plastic tips digging into her skin. Ada took it off and glared at the triceratops. He cowered theatrically. Corey was not the least bit amused. He asked her to try to get Dante Bichette's attention while he was warming up for his turn to hit, but she told him she couldn't then, not until he was through. "Look," Corey said, "it's Don Zimmer."

She should have known that Corey wouldn't want the autograph of a pudgy old-timer, but she wasn't thinking right at the moment. While Ada tried to entice Zimmer to approach Corey, he wheeled himself precariously close to where Dante Bichette stood swinging a weighted bat and started chatting him up, taking another bill out of his pocket.

Ada stormed over. "Are you planning to slip Dante Bichette a twenty?"

"No, of course not," Corey said with a wink.

That was it. Ada started yelling at Corey, screaming at him until she could feel her face grow hot. "Just because you're disabled doesn't mean you should use it to get stuff. That's all you think about, how you can work the wheelchair thing to score more loot, meet famous people, get somebody else to pick up the check." She kept on yelling until she needed to pause for breath. "There are plenty of kids who are really sick, who don't have enough energy to scheme like you do."

"What?" Corey said. He looked as though he had never been hollered at before. "I don't do anything like that. I wish I could run. I didn't ask for any of this. The organizations always approached me. Why are you so mean?" He started choking up. "Nobody has ever been this mean to me before," he gasped, then started to cry.

Ada exhaled all the air in her lungs and her shoulders sank. Corey was a boy too small for his thirteen years with scrawny legs, who had managed to cultivate a vigorous personality and make countless friends. "Oh Corey," Ada said. "I'm so sorry. I mean it." But Corey was rubbing his eyes with his fists and his mother rushed forward and hugged him fiercely.

Ada looked up to see the team's owner sitting in the first row next to the dugout. His mouth was open and his jowls were quivering. She wished she could slink down into the dugout and cower under a pile of sunflower seed shells until everyone had left for the evening. The wood of the dugout floor was soft, cleat-nicked. She could have sunk right into it.

"Don't take your bad day out on my child!" said Corey's mother, who wore a T-shirt with an image of her son's face on it, *My little hero* written in red cursive under his chin.

Ada mumbled more apologies and took a step away from the Pearlmutters.

The centerfielder signed Corey's ball and then paused dramatically and looked at Ada, shook his head and snorted, stopping to whisper something to another player behind his gloved hand before he walked away. *Okay, I yelled at a kid in a wheelchair,* Ada wanted to yell, *but you cheated on your wife with Sherrie!* Ada expected she'd hear from Sherrie about how the players thought she was a raving nut.

Ada somehow led Corey back to his seats, trying to ignore his family's whispers about her—*She must be having boyfriend problems . . . she has no idea what it's like to be disabled*—and to convince herself that what she had done wouldn't turn out that badly—the owner, after all, wasn't Steinbrenner, wasn't Turner. He was a reasonable man. Still, around the office they called him the Big Guy. Ada went to her cubicle and sat with her head in her hands, shaking. A secretary came by and told Ada to report to Chip's office then vanished after issuing the summons.

When Ada walked in his office, her boss was sitting with his chair facing the window.

"I just got a call from the Big Guy," he said. "It seems he saw you yelling at a Care and Share." He swiveled around in his chair and faced her. "What part of Care and Share don't you understand?"

Ada's guts roiled. This was the time she should tell him everything. She should spill every detail of her past illness and save her ass. She should rip open her shirt and display the scars and marks. She should tell her boss that everything could be traced to that, that the cancer had made her crazy, that it had made her mean. It was time for her to say, *Look here, I have an excuse, a better excuse than you've got.*

"You called him an ungrateful charlatan," her boss continued. "His mother has already had someone at Children's Hospital fax over medical records to prove his condition."

"I'm sorry, I'm so sorry," she said, feeling more pathetic than she'd ever felt.

The phone rang and Chip answered it. He looked at Ada and put his hand over the receiver, saying, "I've got to take this," and frowning at her.

Ada walked back to her cubicle and sat down, resting her head on her desk.

"Ada!" Sherrie screamed as she peeked her head over the cubicle's partition. "I thought you'd never stop caring and sharing. So, who are they from?"

"What?"

"The flowers! They came after you walked down to meet the kid."

On the far corner of Ada's desk was a bright bouquet of yellow lilies and red and orange Gerbera daisies in a glass vase. "I don't know," she said, numb. Maybe this was the kiss of death, the owner's way of giving her the axe. Ada reached for the card. She had trouble opening the envelope so Sherrie snatched it from her and took out the card. "They're from Neil!" she squealed.

"Neil?" Ada said, trying to place the name. "You mean Dinger?" When he took off his plush head, Dinger's name was Neil. His face was egg-shaped and his eyes were near-sighted. He had to wear plastic wrap-around glasses underneath the Dinger head so that he didn't crush his usual frames, but they fogged over with sweat so Dinger ran into things without comic intention. When Neil wasn't out mascoting around, he had other duties. Although he was stationed on another floor, he walked by Ada's desk at least once a day. He always managed to find her in the stadium when he was working a game, and once he had come over and sat in her lap to amuse the nearby children. Dinger reeked, absolutely reeked with years of summer mansweat that couldn't be laundered out because the plush costume was difficult to clean. Dinger had smacked her in the face with his stiff purple tail several times and the children laughed.

Ada stood up and looked around to see if anyone else had received flowers from Dinger. He often distributed leftover promotional giveaway items—insulated lunch sacks with the team logo and an advertisement for a brand of vacuum cleaner silk screened on the back, garish plastic checkbook covers with a portrait of the field on one side and a bank's insignia on the other. No one had given Ada flowers in years—not since a raft of bouquets were delivered from Ada's school friends when she first was diagnosed, attention that dwindled to a single lavender rose from Ada's father the day the doctor told her the cancer had gone into remission. What was Ada supposed to say to Dinger? She wondered if he wasn't as smelly when he was out of his costume. Maybe he'd change his mind when word of what Ada had done worked its way through the front office's gossip channels. Maybe the peppy, kid-loving icon of the Rockies would not be allowed to date the dour specimen who'd just lambasted a boy in a wheelchair. But Ada wasn't attracted to Neil. She'd only ever thought of him as a stinky purple triceratops. Was she supposed to pretend that he appealed to her, since she didn't have any other prospects?

"Sherrie," Ada said, "let's go get a drink."

It was comforting to have Sherrie nearby. Reflecting on their mutual depravity consoled Ada, as did Sherrie's cheerful gossip. Ada downed martinis and nodded and said, "No you didn't. You did?" at the proper places in Sherrie's stories until she could barely sit up on the stool and needed to take a cab home. Ada felt close to Sherrie that night because she made absolutely no demands on her.

There wasn't a professional baseball team in Colorado when Ada was growing up and her parents had driven her to Kansas City to see George Brett play on the anniversary of the end of her cancer treatment. By that time people no longer stared at her because her hair had grown back and she didn't look puffy and freakish. She had glossy curls and a ball cap too, a summer tan and a hotdog to eat, and when George Brett hit a homerun the fountains behind centerfield spurted to life. Maybe, she had thought, everything would be better from here on. But that kid hadn't known how hard it would be to continue her life after the treatments and appointments that had ruled it had ended. She wasn't afraid of death after she'd fought it for years, so when her test results came back clean, it was like having a squalling foundling thrust into her lap that she had no idea what to do with. She chose not to think about it. She always figured the relapse would happen, any day now. In the meantime she put one foot in front of the other without deciding anywhere to go. She finished school. She went to the state college. She took the first job she was offered and kept it, simply kept it, making no long-term plans beyond her regular cancer screenings.

Milo finally showed up for a Care and Share at the next afternoon's ballgame, before Ada's boss had a chance to meet with the owner and discuss her behavior. Because they were so busy, firings almost never happened during the season, apart for the sacking of managers who couldn't win, so she had that going for her at least. If she was lucky she probably had until September. Milo's dad called from the phone in the lobby. "I'm sorry I didn't call earlier. He was doing better today and I didn't know how long it would last."

Ada rushed downstairs to meet them. Milo's face had a green tinge, and he slumped in his wheelchair, too weak to respond when Ada talked to him. He wore the jersey of the leftfielder, a pompous man who never signed kids' balls before games. Only Milo's father was with him, a man whose sad eyes were shaded by a John Deere cap. Was Ada fulfilling a last request? She couldn't remember being so young that her last request would have been so simple: to shake a ball player's hand.

Ada led Milo and his father out on the field. Milo looked so sick Ada didn't know what to do. The baseball players bounded around them. They were miracles, prodigies of health, the products of training and discipline and genetics. Their muscles were audacious in formation, daring the beholder not to notice how each one was differentiated from its neighbor, each attuned to perform a singular function. They matched their wives, whom Ada had met at a charity function, unreal cat-suited women, golden and glowing. The first baseman's hands especially amazed Ada, huge shapely instruments that looked as if they originally belonged to an enormous sculpture of a god that was never scaled down to proper size. She approached the players with uncharacteristic boldness, pressing them to sign Milo's ball. When Ada marched up and said, "Will you sign this ball for that kid?" the players all stopped swinging their weighted bats and jogging and chatting and signed Milo's ball, which made Ada think she shouldn't have been so passive with them in the past, obeying the rules for interaction Chip had given her.

The leftfielder was taking batting practice and Milo watched him avidly, without speaking, barely acknowledging the parade of other players who came up to him. "He's not feeling good," his father explained. "Thank you so much." The leftfielder tipped a ball and it careened out behind the batting cage, catching a lip on the field and smacking the bottom of Milo's wheelchair. Ada's heart thrummed fast, and she was relieved that it hadn't hit him. She fished the ball out and Milo looked at it, then up at her, pleading. "Do you want me to get him to sign this ball?" Ada asked. He nodded so vigorously that his thin shoulders participated in the motion. Ada closed her hand around the ball and squeezed it hard as she marched off to corner the leftfielder.

National League RBI leader or no, that bastard was going to sign this ball. She had talked to him once before. He was dumb as a post. Murkily stupid, as though when you looked in his eyes and asked him a question he had to swim up through fathoms of algae-choked water to reach the surface and issue a dim reply. But he was Milo's hero, and so Ada blocked the back entrance into the dugout and thrust the ball and uncapped pen towards him, saying, "Sign, please?" He blinked, then took the pen and signed the ball.

When she gave it to Milo, he cradled it at first, as gently as a soap bubble he never wanted to pop. Ada had spent so much of her life in the company of the sick that this was normal to her: immobile children hunched in chairs, bodies full of unimaginable medicines and chemicals, and this boy, clutching an autographed baseball with weak fingers nearly the same color as the ball.

Ada looked out at the stadium, the thrilling expanse of it, the plentitude of grass and good red dirt. She inhaled deeply, taking in the scent of hot dogs and popcorn and wet grass after light rain. The happy pre-game chatter all around her mingled with the sound of water rushing through the streets outside. Milo, in the middle of it all, held his signed baseball fiercely.

Ada knew that she wasn't a miracle. She and Milo were accidents of their cells, and nothing more. She didn't know what she wanted to do next, but knew it wasn't this. She could no longer shepherd dying children and beg autographs from the famous. She was capable of doing something more than this and she didn't need to be reminded every day about what had happened to her long ago. She could walk away today, resign before her boss had a chance to fire her. And when she came to the ballpark, she would just watch the game. That was the privilege of the well.

Every Happy Family

Reunited, the first thing we think to do is eat. Grandma, three steps ahead of everyone where food is concerned, spreads the table with lavish care. Backyard tomatoes big as melons, sliced thin, horizontally, to best display the divine wisdom in the pattern of their seed-crammed chambers. The melons themselves, big as— well, bigger than melons should be, sunset-colored, succulent, sweet. Roast beef so good, it melts in anticipation of your mouth's heat. Savoring it, we sense the cows that produced it must have been loved to yield up such flavor. Good-looking ears of corn, summer tender, kernels bursting at tooth's touch. And gravy, there will be gravy, fulsome, tawny, flowing from the chipped heirloom server, everlasting. The vessel that contained it not so much a gravy boat as a great china frigate of sauce, sloshing with abundance, three blue flowers on its side, and no matter how much we pour or ladle, coating our plates, filling our stomachs, there is always more.

We eat and eat, and then collapse, frowzy, disoriented, stomachs distended, in front of television, any television, moving instinctively toward the hum. There is always a game on, because it is always some sport's prime season, and one sport is as good as the next, each having its own charm, except for soccer, which isn't spoken of in that house. We look like hell, happy hell, with unwashed hair, sweat-suit clad. Family resemblances the teenagers try to keep at bay through compulsive grooming become apparent then, in the after-gorging lie-about. Then the napping will commence, in all forms, nappers on random couches, napping away contentful afternoons. And in this sort of napping, we don't feel we are taking away from our lives, but adding something to them, being generous, gentle with ourselves, renewing, strengthening, storing this kindly pleasantness for some great trial ahead. There, on Grandma's couches, where laziness is a kind of grace, one hears the healthy snorts and snores of hard-worked people at rest.

And when you wake up from this glorious slumber, you will find your cousin, because in a family with so many, there will be, always, a cousin for you. Your star-intended confidant, from whom you could part and then rejoin in friendship, ages later, without hesitation. First you will steal away from the undesirable cousins, the untouchables in the family caste system, a system fully understood only by you and your cousin. Then, between the two of you, you will find a way to quell the boredom. Two city girls in a little nowhere town, you haunt the second-hand stores, the bowling alley, and the movie theater showing only one film, enjoying the rural quiet of this place.

Then you will rejoin the rest of the tribe and parcel out again into carloads to head to church. Grandmother, proud matriarch, will sit at row's edge, watching the pews fill around her. Look how many pews fill with her family, returned! The ladies Grandma quilts with will cluck over her brood, checking children's rates of growth against recollections of past size, wondering for which granddaughter's welfare they were asked to say ten Hail Marys, each.

After church comes drinking and cards, the uncles popping open cans of cold beer before the aunts even make it out of the cars. The cousins will follow the uncles, the uncles being more fun than the aunts, who liked to assign chores, each uncle funnier than the next, making the cousins laugh until liquids that weren't meant to exit them do. The uncles clomped into Grandma's house, from all corners of the country, leaving, for the moment, jobs in mergers and acquisitions, law, accounting, or engineering. Here, they ate too many peanuts, cracked jokes, and let the cousins sip from their cans. You and your cousin swear you'll never be stuck in the kitchen with the rest of the women until the day you are, a baby on your hip, mashing sweet potatoes just the way he likes it.

The aunts will pair, two by two, to do the dishes and spread the gossip, the Alabama housewife with the New York ad executive, kindred spirits, random friends, brought together by the chance of whom their husband's brother might choose to make his wife. There among the cleansing bubbles, aunts wet up to their elbows, the gossip will commence, innocently, with an offhand remark: the girls, aren't they pretty? Except maybe for Ted and Paula's girl, Sal, but no one mentions this, and the only hint Sal had was that she was never picked to be the flower girl for anyone's wedding. But she was quite the bridesmaid, and she pulled off her duty with proud pink taffeta aplomb, and maybe her skin looked sallow in that shade, and her hips wide in that cut, and maybe the great bright bow served to advertise her rearward dimensions, but her smile: it was radiant. You could see that from afar.

"Look at Sal!" says the chorus of aunts.

Sal, beaming.

"That's a plucky girl," the aunts say, "that girl's got pluck ... and no boyfriend," they add, and they've got to, because they are family after all, gathered only on rare occasions to spread the gossip that keeps the older generations sharp and watchful, keeps them from slipping over the edge, on the lookout for clues.

And what about Joe, the aunts will speculate, Joe, a little slow, his grades not up to family par, but maybe he is handy with a wrench, and is the only one to call when the garbage disposal waxes uncooperative. "Do you hear that Julie has moved in with her boyfriend?" one aunt asks the next, and yes, there still exist families in which such news will cause a stir. Her mother doesn't wish to discuss it, but she will talk about how close Julie is to finishing her law degree. So it goes, with each person carrying within them the seeds of their own redemption, when looked at through kind eyes.

The uncles, their heads beery, their eyes a little wet, will idealize each other, their children, their wives, and they will grab the aunts and kiss them soundly, being too old for concern over the embarrassment of youth.

To take a trip to Grandma's house is to fall into a pit of plenty. Only so many days can we take of this rich living, and when we feel fat and muzzy, super-indulged, loved a little overmuch, that is when we know it is time to clean the house, to leave it as we found it, and head back to our other lives, lives where we have to shower every morning and go for jogs and make a living. And when we wash the gravy boat gently, by hand, we notice the hundred tiny fissures streaming out through the porcelain, but see that not one was strong enough, after all those years of passing and pouring, to make it crack.

The Sit-In

It was the summer of 2017, the country had gone mad, and Jen Novotny derived all her intel about its decline and dim hopes for salvation from a Twitter user called Saber_Seven who claimed to be a former Special Ops agent and posted under the profile picture of a gecko. He told his followers to have faith in the Eagle of Justice. Bobby Three Sticks was on the job, the FinCEN case looked tight, SIGINT on all the treasonweasels abounded, and the menace would soon be stopped. Whenever some new indignity agitated Saber_Seven's followers, he urged them to "stay frosty."

Saber_Seven was probably a hoax, but although the year was only half over, it had been a long one and Jen needed to believe in something again. It might as well be a fucking gecko.

Jen's husband, Devin, said she was getting worked up with the same kind of conspiracy theories she deplored on the other side. One Saturday in June, Jen stirred mac and cheese with a wooden spoon while she thumbed through Facebook on her phone. In secret groups, women plotted their rallies, but on their public pages they clicked the like button on red-state cousins' baby photos. A notification popped up on Jen's screen: "Sit-in for Healthcare!" People were planning to occupy Senator Gardner's eight Colorado offices to protest the healthcare bill. Jen wanted to go. But she'd have to ask Devin first.

"That's rotting your brain," Devin said, startling Jen. He appeared out of nowhere, like a ninja.

"My brain is already rotted," Jen said. Between budget headaches at work, running their twin tween daughters Clementine and Abigail to school, dance, and the orthodontist, endless meetings about their nine-year-old son Freddy's IEP plan and his appointments with various tutors, doctors, and occupational therapists, she needed an outlet for her rage.

As Jen stirred, an ad appeared on her phone for the pencil cases her daughters had asked for, in the shape of smiling, soft-serve poop emoji. Truly, it was a marvel: they were selling these poo cases at regular stores, next to the fidget whatzits the kids were spinning between their fingers nonstop because they could not take the anxiety. Jen remembered a time when to buy anything resembling feces, you had to go to that special joke store in the mall. Now blank-eyed, smiling poo was everywhere. It was the symbol of their times.

Prince was dead and Bowie too. Fires raged across western lands. The coral reefs were skeletized. The oceans lapped ever farther into the coasts. Evil robots had actually overtaken the nation, just like in the wackiest 1950s sci-fi movies, but the robots remained inside the computers, disguised as hot Russian MAGA chicks, so more than half the populace remained unalarmed. Hadn't anyone ever seen *2001?*

"You're fuming about it again," Devin observed. The macaroni began to smoke.

Jen looked up and held out the spoon, covered in artificial cheese. Its febrile tangerine color reminded her of the whole situation. "I'm in the resistance," she said. "I've got to keep informed."

Devin shook his head and smiled sadly. "We don't have enough money in the Health Savings Account for you to see a shrink too."

Of course not. Every penny they could spare had to go toward helping their son.

"Maybe you could take five minutes and do one of those mindfulness podcasts?" Devin suggested. When Freddy was diagnosed with an array of conditions they'd never heard of, Devin turned to yoga and meditation. He practically levitated as he walked around, betraying no emotion.

But Jen believed kids needed emotion. Even if it got them stirred up before bedtime. They had to know what mattered. She knew what she looked like to Devin, to the world. A slightly overweight middle-aged mom with a streak of gray near her right temple, not as any kind of statement but because she only managed to dye her hair twice a year. She didn't look romantic and young like someone in an actual resistance, wearing a beret, Galouises dangling from her lip, her scarf blowing back in the wind of her righteousness. "I'm not crazy," she said, scraping at the macaroni stuck to the bottom of the pan. "The world is."

Devin took the spoon from her and divided the salvageable macaroni between three bowls. "What's the goal? They remove one, you'll get the next one. We've got enough problems here at home."

By problems, he meant Freddy. And he was right. At best, it would be a four-year-grind, if none of the frequent pissing contests with nuke-equipped dictators ended in the big kaboom before then.

Still, Jen didn't like to concede Devin's point. She didn't like to concede anything these days. "We need the health insurance these bastards are trying to take away."

"Bastards!" Freddy echoed from down the hall. His bat ears detected any profanity uttered in his vicinity. Like playing with a new toy, he'd repeat the word for days, at home, at school, in the yard.

Devin shook his head once and made the *calm down* gesture with his hands.

His serenity infuriated Jen. She continued in a whisper, "Without health insurance, we're finished." Jen was the family's Minister of Finance. She calculated everything on the basis of Freddy's $150-an-hour therapy sessions. Taking the family to a movie would cost them half a session. Seventy-five boxes of macaroni equaled one session.

"We have insurance." Devin put the pan into the sink.

"For now." Jen picked a browned noodle out of one bowl. If Freddy saw it he wouldn't eat a bite. "They're talking about reinstating lifetime limits. And Medicaid—what if Freddy needs it someday when we can't take care of him?"

"You're catastrophizing," Devin said.

Freddy, Mr. Pre-Existing Condition himself, walked in. "Something smells bad," he said. Freddy's copper-gold hair was eye-catching enough to draw strangers in to comment, who then quickly retreated after talking to him. His light eyelashes and freckled skin had given him an elfin look until he was about seven, when he grew stocky and strong—nobody's sprite.

"What do you mean?" Jen said, forcing a smile. She opened a window to let in some air. She spent half her life cooking Freddy's odd, specific food, and the other half convincing him not to reject it.

Freddy bent his head low to the bowl and sniffed. "I'm not eating this." He stood, adding, "Bastards," before he went back to his iPad.

When she tried to imagine Freddy grown up, selecting a meal at a college dining hall or office cafeteria, she couldn't. She had no idea if he'd ever leave them or if he'd be like that man with Down Syndrome she saw walking in the evenings with his ninety-year-old father, a skin-and-bones specter who'd somehow determined not to die. You didn't get to rest until the future seemed secure for your kids, and right now the calendar with the future on it bore a giant, smiling poop emoji. While Clementine and Abigail ate, Jen went online to learn more about the sit-in. She had to make Devin understand its importance.

"Ignore all #provokatsiya, patriots. Only you can save this democracy," Saber_Seven tweeted. She looked up the Russian word. It meant staged provocations intended to stoke resentments for political advantage. That just sounded like life these days, everyone ginned up in a perpetual state of alarm, responding to manufactured emergencies meant to distract from the real ones.

That night in bed, Jen whispered to Devin. "A bunch of people are planning sit-ins at Senator Gardner's offices this week, to protest the health care bill. I want to go with them."

"Peaceful sit-ins?"

"Of course."

"On Saturday? Sure, I can watch the kids while you do that."

"No, the offices aren't open on the weekends. It has to be during the week."

"But we need those Paid Time Off days."

As the lesser breadwinner, Jen used most of her vacation days for Freddy—to go to his appointments and watch him on bad days. "This is important. If the bill passes, we'll have worse problems than no vacation."

"For someone who catastrophizes constantly, you're surprisingly optimistic about your ability to influence a senator."

Jen's neck muscles tightened a notch. "Can you get the kids after camp on Tuesday?"

"I have a presentation. A meeting."

"Thanks. You'll juggle. The idea is to attract publicity about what's in this healthcare bill. They're releasing it less than a week before they vote. We need to shame them."

"You'd be good at that." Devin flipped over on his pillow and switched off his reading lamp.

Decades ago Jen had been an A student. Praised by teachers and parents. Her school portraits framed in gold, draped with ribbons she'd won. Devin used to tell her how irresistible she was. Now the only feedback she got was negative. "You're damn right I would," Jen said, daring to raise her voice to a normal speaking volume.

Freddy screamed from his bedroom across the hall. "You woke me up! Bastards!"

Devin let out air like he was deflating.

Jen grabbed a bottle of chamomile-lavender spray and went to appease Freddy. She had never been more essential and less appreciated. What if she died? You'd have to hire five workers to replace what she did for this family. If you zapped all these ordinary mothers out of the world, everything in motion that they kept on track would collide and burst into flames. In fact, the country was beginning to resemble what happened when moms were not in charge.

Before Jen left for the sit-in Tuesday morning, Freddy couldn't find the only shoes he agreed to wear to camp, so she rushed to arrive for the opening of the Fort Collins office, near where she lived. She sped a little, wanting to make the most of the day she'd taken off work. She wove through traffic and parked in the strip mall lot she was surprised to find so empty. Where was everybody? Maybe they'd carpooled. "Stay frosty," she told herself as she opened the door to the office building between a Kumon and a SoulCycle.

As Jen mounted the stairs, she quoted the gecko quoting Sun Tzu: "The opportunity to secure ourselves against defeat lies in our own hands, but the opportunity of defeating the enemy is provided by the enemy himself."

The brass nameplate glinted in the light of a window at the end of the hall. Senator Gardner's office. Over the past year, she'd called this man more often than she'd ever called a boyfriend, relative, or friend. She talked to his voicemail and occasionally one of his staffers. She always began her call, "Hello, I'm a constituent," because he'd told a reporter that most of the people who contacted him were paid protestors from New York and California. He'd ignored her requests as assiduously as if he bore her a personal grudge.

Fear fluttered in her stomach. So far most of her activism had been virtual. But for Freddy's sake she needed to be brave and support the others protesting in person.

The windowless reception area was empty. An unoccupied desk stood next to a door to another room. A phone with lights blinking red and white sat unanswered. Two worn office chairs hugged the wall under a glossy photograph of Pike's Peak. Had she gotten the date wrong?

The door to the back room opened and a young man emerged, blowing on a Styrofoam cup of coffee. Slim and thin-necked, his dark hair had an unctuous sheen like he was part weasel, and his skin was so pale he might have lived in a terrarium. "Oh, hello," he said, sounding startled by her presence. "May I help you?"

"I'd like to speak to Senator Gardner, please," she said. "I'm a constituent. It's about the healthcare bill."

"Senator Gardner isn't in, Ma'am."

"Is he ever in?" She'd grown to loathe the smug, silver-haired gerbil of a man who'd narrowly won the election a few years earlier. *Comparing humans to animals is part of how we got in this mess*, Devin would say sagely, citing historical examples. *Don't call a senator a gerbil.*

"Senator Gardner visits from time to time," he said.

"Are there other constituents back there?" Of course, they must already be assembled in a conference room.

He raised his eyebrows, puzzled. "No, Ma'am. You're the first today."

Jen sank into a chair and checked Facebook. Digging back through the comments, it appeared that sometime between when she'd started Freddy's occupational therapy exercises the night before—helping him lie on his stomach and move his head in the opposite direction of the arms he alternately stuck out, one hundred times—and that morning's shoe incident, the plan had changed. Instead of simultaneously occupying the senator's eight Colorado offices, they'd decided to converge on the Denver office.

Jen clicked over to the livestream of the group's most famous activist, Cat Cha, the rapper/frontwoman of a local hip-hop group who used a wheelchair due to a genetic condition and frequently headlined the Taste of Colorado. It looked like a carnival at the Denver office. Tents covered the lawn outside the looming buildings. People in yellow shirts, sun hats, walkers and wheelchairs pumped signs on which the grim reaper wore a red baseball hat. Was she supposed to have worn a yellow shirt? Or brought a sign?

She messaged a mom she'd met at the Women's March who'd gone to Denver—her daughter had a heart condition. She explained the mishap and asked for instructions. "Let me check," Jen's friend wrote.

A few minutes later, a message from Cat Cha appeared on Jen's screen: "Hold the Fort."

"Are u sure?" Jen tapped back, awed. She'd never actually communicated with Cat directly.

"Absolutely." Cat Cha wrote. "We've got Denver. U get FC. I'll try to send some people up."

An assignment. She'd been given an assignment. Their group was ragtag and ad hoc, existing mostly just to let them vent, spurred onward by whoever had more energy or time or anger that week. But now she'd been given a specific task by the closest person they had to a leader, a bona fide rap star.

"Roger Wilco," Jen typed back, as she imagined Saber_Seven would have. She stared at the young man, organizing the papers on the desk, and meditated on not thinking of him as a weasel, greedily hoarding all the eggs, even the meager ones that symbolized Freddy's slim chances in life. She'd only been here three minutes and already her metaphors were out of control.

He looked up at Jen. "I'd be happy to take your message and give it to Senator Gardner—he's really not due in."

"I'll wait," Jen said. "We're doing a sit-in."

"We?"

"Most of us ended up going to Denver. But more will be here soon."

"I don't know what that's going to accomplish, Ma'am. It's just me here."

"I'll wait until the senator comes to speak to us."

"Suit yourself," he said, picking up the phone and playing constituents' voicemails. Screaming, tinny and quiet, but unmistakable, came from the handset.

Her name was Jennifer, the single most popular name given to (mostly white) girls born in America between 1970 and 1984. It was not only the white women who had done this to the country, but that was the group Jen blamed most. According to exit polls, fifty-two percent of them had voted for the Cheeto. A similar percentage of Jens, Jennies, and Jennifers had presumably voted for him. The thought made her sick. Jen wanted to change her name. To Xena. To Prudence. To an unpronounceable symbol. Perhaps a poop emoji.

Forty percent of Americans were A-OK with everything, had pulled the lever for that guy and then resolutely looked away. A similar percentage of people dropped their dogs' bagged shit along the side of trails with the alleged, never fulfilled intention of retrieving and discarding it on their way back.

And this young man was one of them.

"May I ask your name?" Jen said when the young man stopped answering the phone to perform some neck-limbering exercises. A name would help her stop thinking of him as a weasel. *Remember, we're all human,* Zen Devin said in her head.

"Tristan," he said.

"Nice to meet you," she said, "I'm Jen," remembering her manners like she always told Freddy to. "Are you enjoying your coffee?" Some fraction of her tax money probably supplied it.

"It's not bad. Do you want some?"

"Thanks, I've got mine." She held up the metal travel coffee mug that she'd bought to economize, writing Starbucks out of their budget to save up for EpiPens, priced as though gold-plated. She wouldn't be accepting food or drink here. She wouldn't make Persephone's mistake. "Do you need help answering the phones?" She thought of all those mothers, waiting to be heard. Disclosing their lupus and their kids' dialysis bills in the vague hope that it would matter. She wanted to give them a warm human voice instead of the chilly draft of the senator's chipper recorded greeting.

Tristan chuckled. "Thanks, but only trained staff can. Things can get a little heated."

"I wonder why that would be?" Jen said.

Tristan's lips drew taut. "How is your sit-in going? I checked the news—it looks like everyone is in Denver."

"Reinforcements will be here."

"Sure," Tristan said.

Almost two hours in, Jen needed to use the bathroom down the hall. She'd stocked her cavernous purse with wet wipes, protein bars for the aging woman's nutritional needs, a sweatshirt in case she got chilly, her phone charger, stacks of medical forms to fill out so Freddy could go to summer camp, and a draft of a code infrastructure document that was due next week at work. But she didn't bring a port-a-potty.

"You're not going to lock this door behind me when I leave for a moment, are you?" she asked.

"Why would I do that?" Tristan asked. "We're open until five every weekday. But, like I said, the senator's not coming." He lowered his voice like he was letting her in on some private information. "I'd be surprised if he visits even once this summer. You could make more productive use of your time."

"I want a meeting. He met with those healthcare executives. Why won't he meet with people his votes affect?"

"I know!" Tristan said, his expression eager. "I'll put you on the priority list for the Senator's next telephone town hall."

Jen snorted. "I'll be back in a minute."

When she returned, Jen checked on the rally in Denver. A mariachi band played. Someone had wheeled in a cotton candy machine. A group of ten protestors had moved from the staging grounds outside the building into Gardner's office. Stocked with takeout from Starbucks, they'd set up camp next to his office flag, posting signs and demands on the walls around them. Jen clicked from one person's livestream to the next and yearned to be there. She messaged Cat Cha: "Nobody else here. Should I join u guys in Denver?"

After a while, Cat replied, "Naw. The Fuzz told us fire regs say only 10 can occupy the office. I sent some people to FC. Stay strong, Sister."

The prospect of others arriving heartened Jen. They needed her to hold the Fort. At least for this one day she'd taken off work.

She turned on her laptop. She'd expected to be too busy with solidarity and camaraderie to work, but that plan, like pretty much every plan she'd made during adulthood, didn't turn out as expected.

"WiFi password?" she asked Tristan, who was rubbing his temples. The calls must have been giving him a headache. His standard refrain, *The senator hasn't yet taken a position on the issue. I'll be sure to let him know your concerns,* had begun to take on a careworn singsong.

Tristan laughed. "I don't think so."

"Fine," she said. He'd probably been instructed to make things inhospitable so she'd leave. She used her phone to set up a MiFi hotspot, plugging all the devices into the outlet by Tristan's desk.

"Uh, I might need to use that outlet."

"I'm just using a little taxpayer electricity. I'll make room if need be."

Later, after a lunch of one SheRa energy bar, a Gecko alert popped onto Jen's screen. The Senate had delayed the procedural vote on the bill for a week, until after Independence Day.

Jen checked in with Denver. "Does this mean we leave?" she asked on the group chat.

"No!" Cat Cha answered. "We stay until Gardner agrees to speak with us and pledges to vote against the bill."

"When will the others be here?" Jen asked.

"Soon!"

"What do I do when the office closes?" Jen asked.

"Lie down on the floor!" Cat Cha responded. "I want you to send me a selfie of your smiling face before you go to bed! You're doing awesome! You are a brave and formidable woman!"

Jen hadn't expected to stay the night. She thought other people would pull the gung-ho duty. But maybe Devin should skip his evening yoga and take the bedtime shift for once. Still, her hips were already starting to ache from her chronically tight IT bands. She practically needed to sleep on a full-body feather pillow. But the activists in Denver would be sleeping in their wheelchairs. She couldn't tell Cat Cha she had to go home because she didn't have a toothbrush. If they could endure that, Jen could do this. Freddy might not complete his OT exercises for Devin. But Devin needed to learn what it felt like to try. "Roger Wilco," Jen typed.

At 4:30, Jen used the facilities and refilled her water bottle.

Tristan emerged from the back office, smiling. "They're delaying the vote," he said. "You got your way. You can leave."

"I learned that two hours ago," Jen said. Senator Gardner probably didn't keep Tristan informed. That way Tristan could honestly say the senator hadn't taken a position on the issue yet— for all Tristan knew, he hadn't. "We stay until this bill is pulled. Me, and the reinforcements who should be arriving soon."

Tristan produced a noise of exasperation surprisingly similar to the sound that Devin often made in reference to her. Perhaps this sound could be her new name. "I was going to a concert tonight!"

Jen smiled. "I'll be your concert, Tristan." She began singing "We Shall Overcome," her voice wobbling around the notes as Tristan paced the office. She'd never sung it alone before. When she got to "We'll walk hand in hand, some day," she looked directly at Tristan, half hoping he'd join in.

"I'm calling my supervisor," he said, and scuttled into the back room.

Would the supervisor tell Tristan to call the cops? Maybe she should leave. The Fort Collins office appeared to be minimally staffed—it could be that Tristan had no backup, and as long as Jen was in, he was in too. He was too young to care about healthcare, but if he suffered a little, maybe he would think, for at least a moment, about the people this bill would hurt.

Jen wrangled Devin on the phone, keeping her voice low so Tristan wouldn't hear.

"I'm needed here," she told him.

"What makes you think that?"

"They told me they needed me." *Which is more than you ever say, Mr. Self-Contained.*

Devin let a chilly silence sit between them. "All right," he said finally.

That evening Jen hunkered in the corner, answering demanding texts from her family, and posting a selfie, smiling from the nest she'd fashioned out of some GARDNER FOR COLORADO T-shirts. She got four likes, one heart, and one laughing face. At dinnertime, three of Tristan's friends arrived with a pizza: two young women with long hair, and a guy who looked happy to be left alone with both of them. They smelled of night air and wore tight concert clothes, eager to see something called Post Malone. Freddy would never know such freedom. They studied Jen like she was a hysterical freak who'd trapped their friend with her hormonal demands. "So this is the lady?" a blonde with wide-set eyes asked Tristan.

"Yeah," he said. "I have to stay here with her. My boss said not to call the cops yet. They'll decide what to do about all the protestors tomorrow."

"*All* of them?" The girl smirked.

"There are more, in Denver," Tristan said. "All extra staff is handling that situation."

"And there will be more here," Jen said.

"Not tonight, there won't," Tristan said, "with the outside door locked."

Jen's spirits sank. Slumber party for one it was. But at least no cops yet.

"Why don't you just leave, lady?" the redheaded girl said. "This protest—or whatever—is so stupid."

"Yeah, where's your vagina hat?" the blonde asked.

"Hey," Tristan said, "keep it civil."

"You're too young to realize this," Jen said, sounding momish, she knew, "but most people aren't at liberty to *just leave* when things get tough."

The girls barely stifled their laughter and disappeared quickly with the other boy. Jen and Tristan sat silently staring at each other. He made a show of eating the pizza in front of her, its cheesy aroma wafting over. Jen unwrapped her second SheRa bar of the day with a loud crinkle. After eating, Tristan retired to his back office, turning the light off there, Jen could see through the glazed window, but leaving on the light in her portion of the office, its buzzing so loud she stuffed in the earplugs she kept in her purse to use whenever Freddy wouldn't stop screaming.

For a few hours, Jen stretched out and enjoyed the luxury of no one needing her. But at eight o'clock, she would have begun Freddy's elaborate bedtime ritual at home and felt a pang. Devin texted her questions, his terse messages displaying no Zen. Maybe he'd appreciate her more after she was gone for a night. No, ploys like that only worked on TV. What if Devin was right, and nothing Jen did mattered, and she'd sacrificed a night with her family to this sad, lonely campout? But if all was lost, and Freddy's care eroded, at least she'd know she'd tried everything she could. And that's who Jen was. A tryer. Despite one disappointment after another, if she stopped trying she'd cease to be herself.

On Wednesday morning, Jen woke in excruciating back pain to the text, "Dad doesn't know where leotards R." Gymnastics camp started today. She texted the twins the precise location.

"Thanx. Where R U?"

"Exercising my first amendment rights." No response after that. The twins always fled when she talked politics.

When Tristan came out from the back office, looking slightly disheveled from the night, to unlock the front door, Jen looked up with hope, but no one waited to get in. Jen ate a rationed breath mint. Cat Cha texted, saying some people were trying to make it up later that day—there was something wrong with a carburetor—and Jen called work to burn another PTO day. Jen's boss trusted her because she always made up for the time she missed and her absences gave him leverage. "I've got to stay one more day," Jen told Devin when he called.

"Freddy's unraveling because you're not here for his routine," he said.

The bedtime routine was Jen's masterpiece, a formula she'd perfected over the years to achieve the most potential calm. First, OT exercises. Then she swung him back and forth on his rolling office chair, pulling on his toes the way he liked it. Twenty minutes of bedtime stories. Three specific songs, in precise order, in her scratchy voice. His stuffed eagle perched in a rolled-up blanket nest. The whole thing took at least an hour. Clementine and Abigail complained she never had time to help them with homework. Possibly all her kids would grow up to call her a bastard.

Freddy wailed in the background, yelling *Dumbass Bastards Shit!*

"Freddy sounds normal," Jen said. "How are you doing?"

"I'm doing well," Devin said, but there was an edge to his voice that reminded her of when she met him, when he used to cuss at cars that cut him off and didn't project a sheen of calm all the time.

"Can you hold on just a little bit longer?" Jen asked. "I think we have a chance. They delayed the vote and look at the news." All across the country, people were sitting in. Raising a ruckus. Speaking their minds.

"So this is like a spiritual retreat for you," Devin said.

Jen could smell her own armpits. "Yeah, all this office needs is an essential oil diffuser."

Devin agreed to one more day, one more night if necessary. Jen hoped the protest would reach some kind of crisis point by then, so she wouldn't have to just slink off, defeated. If she took another PTO day her boss would make her pull Christmas duty again.

Tristan came and went, answering phone calls with his standard line, opening mail, filing papers, ignoring Jen. At 4:45, after her last-of-the-day visit to the facilities, she got a text from Devin.

"WHY AREN'T YOU HERE???? BE HOME AT 8!!!! BASTURD!"

"I love you too, Freddy," she texted back. She wanted to tell him that she was doing this for him. Because she loved him and because he deserved a chance to live as well as possible. But he'd never understand. What use was a loving gesture when it was never reciprocated, and perhaps never even felt? She loved, whether or not it was returned, because she was human. She spoke up, whether or not her words were heeded, because she was a citizen.

Tristan's friends showed up with another pizza at dinnertime. They asked why the cops hadn't taken Jen away and Tristan said, "Senator Gardner says he hopes the situation will resolve itself peacefully. And that staff has to stay as long as the protesters do." He spoke with a terse cadence that made Jen wonder if Tristan was mocking the senator.

Tristan asked his friends about their boring days interning with accountants and mutual fund managers. "So did you get those invoices out in time?" he asked, desperate to convince them to stay.

She wanted to tell Tristan, in her experience, when you faced trouble, friends deserted you. Even family didn't want to see the whole truth. She'd hosted parties when Freddy was younger, but Freddy got so agitated that she'd spend the whole night trying to calm him down. So she stopped inviting people. And they stopped inviting her. The bonds between the other parents at school seemed stronger than the connections she made with them between rushing off to various appointments. She'd see them on Halloween, walking down the street drinking from red cups of spiked punch from pre-trick-or-treating parties that she hadn't been invited to while she marched Freddy around their cul-de-sac alone. Jen was marked, isolated. That's why she hadn't quit Facebook when she'd learned about its betrayals. She didn't want to be alone again. And she was Freddy's link to the world, so she had to keep fighting for the country to allow him a place in it.

But Jen was used to fighting alone. She was good at it. She texted Cat Cha: "Nobody else wants to come to FC, right? But it's okay. I've got this."

Cat Cha replied with a thumbs-up emoji.

As the door closed behind Tristan's friends, the smile faded from his face. Tristan's hair gel had loosened its hold. The armpits of his once-crisp blue Oxford shirt were sweaty. The phone kept ringing until he silenced it for the night. Even with the sound off, it had to alarm him to be staring down a flashing phone day after day, and to have his ear screamed off when he answered it.

"You're not getting paid enough for this," Jen said.

"That may be, but I'm not quitting."

"No, I didn't mean that you should quit. I just meant—you're not doing this for the money or power. Obviously. You're being a public servant. And I respect that."

"Okay," Tristan said. He sank into his chair and folded his hands on the pizza box. "If I'm being a public servant, then I should listen to your story. They've all got a story." He gestured toward a stack of notes, faxes, and letters.

Jen told him about Freddy. About how he couldn't go outside after it rained because he dreaded the smell of mashed worms on the sidewalk. About how they couldn't cuss around him because he'd repeat the words, and so he'd never learned the grammar of swearing that one would soak up from a fluent cussing household. "One time he said, 'You guys are a hell in the butt!'"

"That's quite an indictment." He glanced at the greasy pizza box. "Do you want some?"

Jen thought of Persephone. "No, I shouldn't take your food."

"Come on, you must be starving."

Jen's stomach growled, wanting its say in the decision. "Okay, only if we trade. Here, have a SheRa bar." It was Jen's second-to-last provision.

Tristan took it. "These things have soy and estrogen in them, right?"

"That's right. Take a bite and I'll have to milk you at dawn."

"Okay," Tristan said, handing her a slice.

"You first," she said. She watched him unwrap the bar and take a tentative nibble before she devoured her pizza. She asked Tristan about himself and he told her he was a student at Colorado State, an economics major and treasurer of the Young Republicans.

"Do you want to go into politics?" she asked.

"I'd like to contribute in some way, but I'm not sure. I'm not the kind of guy who inspires confidence in people."

Jen detected the telltale signs of rejection on Tristan—the gray shadows under his eyes, the slouch of his slim shoulders. "You applied for this job in DC, didn't you?"

He shrugged. "I probably wouldn't have made it in a big city like that anyway."

"Don't sell yourself short," Jen said. "This group I'm in—it's helped me with my confidence."

"This group that left you high and dry?"

That was one way to look at it. Another way was that they'd trusted her to handle this protest herself. "Tristan, you're just a Young Republican. That means you can still grow and change."

"Ma'am, I'm from the Western Slope. You city people don't understand us. You look down on us."

"Oh please," Jen said. "I grew up around Republicans. When I was a kid, I raised a steer, Slappy, who was the blue ribbon 4-H champion four years running." She'd done no such thing.

A smile twitched on Tristan's face. "Slappy, huh?"

Jen worried she'd told an obvious lie. But she'd only lied to show Tristan how close they truly were. "Look," she said, "all I'm here for is my son. Rural people have kids, and bodies. And if you have a body, one day it will betray you. Surely we can agree on that."

"Health insurance is expensive, but you know, we don't have endless money."

Jen smiled. This felt like the old ballgame between his side and hers, when they used to keep things in bounds and play as though they still had to sit in the classroom with each other the next day. Maybe she couldn't nudge his thinking one millimeter toward her perspective. But here they were, talking in a way that Jen probably never would with her own son.

That night Tristan turned off the light in her part of the office, and it felt like an extravagant gesture of kindness.

On Thursday morning, Jen woke at seven a.m. to a texted string of poop emoji. It could have been sent by any number of people in Jen's life. Jen's hair was greasy and her breath stank. She must have looked like a gorgon.

On the livestream, police were arresting the protestors in Denver. A woman with cerebral palsy was lying on the floor chanting, "Rather go to jail than die without Medicaid!" as they zip-tied her hands and carried her down to a waiting van. Cat Cha was the last to be rounded up. She spoke to her camera. "Without attendant services from Medicaid, we'd be locked away in institutions until we died." She held her fist in the air, the knuckles of her right hand tattooed with R I O T, before the cops restrained her and the live feed ceased. Was that it? Should Jen leave now? Would they arrest Jen too, or was her protest too small to register?

Tristan emerged from the back room, his eyes tired and his hair sticking up. "My supervisor called the police on you ten minutes ago for trespassing. If you leave now, you won't be arrested."

Jen felt flattered. Someone had noticed her. Maybe it was selfish to push it all the way to getting arrested. It would burn another PTO day. There'd be a fine—who knew how many therapy sessions it would cost. Devin would disapprove. Jen never wasted time, energy, or money. But she missed the luxury of wastefulness.

Six months earlier, Jen had spent hours making signs with Abigail and Clementine for the Women's March on a bright, warm January day. A friend knitted Jen a pink hat. When they discovered all the buses to Denver were full, a group of ten of them threw in $40 a piece and rode in a limousine. They asked the driver to drop them a few blocks away—limousine rides probably weren't in keeping with the spirit of the march. More than 100,000 people thronged the streets, everyone cheering and chanting, thanking the police officers along the route, nobody pushing even when their bodies bottlenecked. For one day, Jen had felt joyful, and so much less alone. But the Women's March was just the fife-and-drum prelude. This was the actual war. It was a battle for her son's right to a dignified existence. And it was so simple—all she had to do was stay here.

Tristan looked out the window in the main office. "The cops are coming."

"I'm ready." *Stay frosty*, she told herself.

"Come on, Jen," Tristan said, a worried crease on his forehead. "There's no media here. All the reporters are in Denver. You'll be lucky if you get a one-line mention in the back of the *The Coloradoan*. You don't want an arrest on your record."

"An official record of my existence sounds kind of nice, actually."

Tristan shook his head. "What exactly is your plan?"

"Let your plans be dark and impenetrable as night, and when you move, fall like a thunderbolt."

"*The Art of War*, right? That's like my favorite book. After *The Fountainhead*."

"There's where we differ."

"Who will take care of Freddy if you get arrested?"

"I don't know." She didn't comfort him by saying it would probably be a catch-and-release misdemeanor. She was enjoying his concern too much. And who knew how this day would turn out, or how any of them would?

"Aren't you afraid?" Tristan asked.

"All of life is unknown. Sometimes you've just got to leap out into that void." She sounded like Devin. "And Tristan, I don't think of you as a weasel anymore."

"Oh," he said. "Thanks?"

"But that doesn't mean I think you're right. You've been lucky. You were born safe. And no matter how you plan and save and delay gratification, luck doesn't always last."

"You sound like a mom."

"There's nothing shameful about taking care of each other."

Heavy footfalls approached from down the hall. Would the police drag her up from the floor? She decided to stand. Her knees trembled. Would the handcuffs hurt?

She wanted to run, but instead she did what she'd been doing ever since she had kids: pretending she was not afraid. "Watch me, Tristan. This is what a mom sounds like. Here," she said, handing him her phone and turning on her own livestream, "Can you record this for me?"

"I guess," he said.

Jen's hands sweated as the two officers entered the room, her home for the past three days. She glanced at the camera Tristan trained on her. She closed her eyes and pictured Freddy at twenty, with prospects as bright as Tristan's, at forty, with his life full of obligation. She threw her fist in the air and chanted "Healthcare for all!" before they tightened the zip-tie around her wrists and the plastic cut into her flesh. No one that cared could hear her. But this was Jen's moment, even if nobody saw it.

"Wait," Tristan said as the cops began to march Jen away. "There's something you should know."

She waited for him to tell her that he'd changed his mind, that she was right.

He leaned close to whisper. "The purple ribbon is the top prize in 4-H, not the blue."

"Oh," Jen said. "Thanks."

"Slappy deserves the best." Tristan winked at her and then tucked her phone into her purse.

That summer, women across the country would post pictures of their children's chests, scarred from heart surgery, and photos of themselves, bald from chemo. Senator Gardner would vote yes on the healthcare repeal, but Senator John McCain, his eyebrow scabbed from surgery on the brain tumor that would kill him in a year, turned his thumb down to defeat the bill. In August, Nazis marching in Charlottesville, Virginia, would kill a young woman. The next summer, border agents would separate children from their parents and detain the kids in concrete and chain-link pens. The next fall, a rally-riled man with pictures of his leader plastered over a van would dispatch pipe bombs to a hit list. Others would defile a newsroom, a grocery store, a synagogue, and a Walmart. Meditation apps could not ease the dread.

As Jen rode in the back of the squad car, she thought about how there was no guarantee this country would continue to be the land of the free. There was no guarantee Freddy would grow up to have something resembling a normal life—or that Clementine or Abigail would. And since there was no such guarantee, there was no reason for Jen to continue to behave in exchange for a vague promise of a happy ending. Instead, she could become something unpleasant, plopped in plain view, declining to budge, refusing to let you forget the ways in which you'd disappointed her.

Acknowledgments

The first person I thought of when I learned this story collection would be published was my teacher, mentor, and friend, Lucia Berlin, who I consider to be one of the all-time best short story writers. I wrote four of these stories in her workshop, and all of them with her wisdom and encouragement in my heart. I am grateful to Joe Wilkins, J. Bruce Fuller, and all the people at the Texas Review Press for selecting *Mixed Company* for the George Garrett Fiction Prize. My writing group, which meets at Murphy's in Boulder when there's no global pandemic happening, is so instrumental to my writing, sanity, and happiness that my husband once asked me, "Don't you write your stories by committee?" Jennifer Sullivan Corkern (aka Sully), Erika Krouse, Rachel Weaver, and Paula Younger are four of the best writers and people I know and I owe them the next round and a whole lot more. Thanks to Gessy Alvarez, Ashley Simpson Shires, Steve Caldes, Greg Glasgow, Cat Altman Kurtz, Doug Kurtz, and Kate Jenkins who helped me with early drafts of these stories. I'm grateful to the editors at the publications in which these stories first appeared, especially Andrew Tonkovich of the *Santa Monica Review*, who published two of these stories and regaled me with tales of his lettuce boycott sit-in days, and Gregory Wolfe, the founder of *Image*, who published my work and selected me to be a Mullin Scholar in the Generations in Dialogue program at the University of Southern California, where I benefited from the insights of my friends Lisa Ampleman, Dave Griffith, Samuel Martin, Brian Volck, and Kathleen Witkowska Tarr. Thank you to David Hicks, who hired me for the best job in the world, teaching in the Mile High MFA Program at Regis University, my program directors Andrea Rexilius and Eric Baus, and my inspiring colleagues and students. Love to Mom, Dad, Jonathan, Whitney, Payton, JT, Thomas (aka Coach), Jordan, Anasa, Lizzy, Jilly, Betty, and all the Chastangs, Shanks, and Hottovys. Julien, Maya, Theo, and Floppy, my office rabbit, I've spent over a year in quarantine with you and I'm still not tired of your company. Now kids, if you've read this far, go practice your instruments.

"*L'homme de ma vie*" appeared in the April 2016 issue of *Barrelhouse* and received Special Mention in the *2018 Pushcart Prize XLII*.

"Lightest Lights Against Darkest Darks" appeared in the Winter 2009 issue of *Prairie Schooner*.

"Casa del Rey" appeared in the Spring 2012 issue of *Santa Monica Review*.

"Moonlight, Starlight, Boogie Won't Be Out Tonight," appeared in the Winter 2010 issue of *Alaska Quarterly Review*.

"La Sexycana" appeared in the *Chicago Tribune*'s *Printer's Row* in June 2015.

"Last Summer's Song" appeared in the Summer 1999 issue of *Michigan Quarterly Review* and was listed among the Notable Essays of 1999 in the *Best American Essays 2000*.

"Hurts" appeared in the Summer 2000 issue of *Weber Studies: The Contemporary West*.

"Local Honey" appeared in the Spring 2005 issue of *Michigan Quarterly Review*.

"Signing for Linemen" appeared in *Five Chapters* in January 2014.

"Community Relations" appeared in the Summer 2006 issue of *Image*.

"Every Happy Family" placed third in *Glimmer Train*'s Very Short Fiction Award and was excerpted there and appeared in its entirety in the Spring 2002 issue of *Eureka Literary Magazine*.

"The Sit-In" appeared in the Spring 2021 issue of *Santa Monica Review*.

The George Garrett Fiction Prize

highlights one book a year for excellence in a short story collection or novel.

Previous Winners

William Black, *In the Valley of the Kings*
Susan Lowell, *Two Desperados*
Jim Kelly, *Pitchman's Blues*
James Ulmer, *The Fire Doll*
Jeff P. Jones, *Love Give Us One Death*
Kathy Flann, *Get A Grip*
Stephen March, *The Gold Piano*
Tim Parrish, *The Jumper*
Starner Jones, *Purple Church*
David Armand, *The Pugilist's Wife*
Richard Spilman, *The Estate Sale*
Mary Kuykendall-Weber, *River Roots*
Jack Smith, *Hog To Hog*
Meg Moceri, *Sky Full of Burdens*
Jacqueline Bautista, *Fiestas*
Gail Mount, *Pitching Tents*
Mark Brazaitis, *An American Affair*
Steve Sherwood, *Hardwater*
John Cottle, *The Blessings of Hard-Used Angels*
Thomas Cobb, *Acts of Contrition*
Naton Leslie, *Marconi's Dream and Other Stories*
Roger Hart, *Erratics*
Don Meredith, *Wing Walking*
Peter Leach, *Tales of Resistance*